A LOOK THROUGH MY EYES:

Unexplainable Ghost Experience

Based on True Events

TYINA SHARP HOPKINS

ISBN
978-1-957378-84-8 (Paperback)
978-1-957378-83-1 (eBook)
978-1-957378-85-5 (Hardcover)

Table of Contents

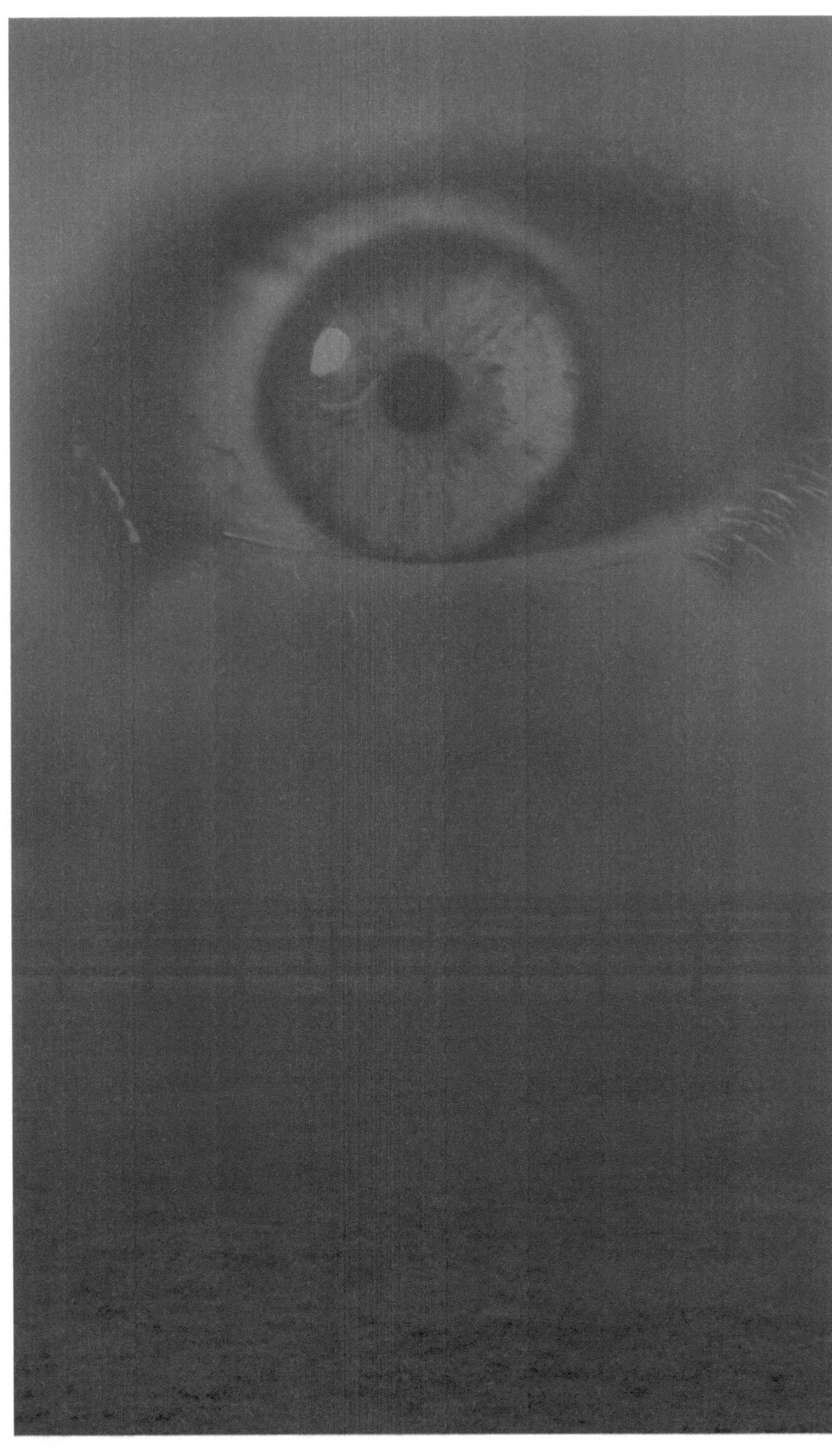

About the author

WRITING THIS BOOK HAS GIVEN ME an opportunity to share some strange but, true events that has been reoccurring in my life since my childhood. First let me tell you a little bit about myself.

My name is Tyina Sharp Hopkins aka Chantel Love, the author of my first book Truth Be Told. I was born in Alabama during the year of 1962. However, I was raised in Philadelphia. My parents would take my sister and I on vacation and we would travel by car and it was the longest trip ever. My sister and I did want to stay there no longer than a week, because we would hear and see inexplicable things or let me just say me, because she had reservation about spirits. My grandparents resided on 50 or more acers of land. The land my grandparents live on they raise farm animals and vegetables. Also, my grandparents had several homes built on their secluded land that aunts and uncles lived in. However, this where I started to witness for myself about Supernatural Demonic Spirits and about the spirits that are unharmful.

I Tyina Sharp Hopkins aka Chantel Love, is ready to invite you into my Demonic, Supernatural Spiritual, and Mythological World. I hope you enjoy my book and know you are not alone in the Mythology about Supernatural Spirits.

Preface

I AM WRITING THIS BOOK TO tell you about the true events that I, Tyina Sharp Hopkins aka Chantel Love, have had and continue to have, from my childhood years up to my current adult years. My family is originally from Alabama. My father was born there, my mother grew up there, and my grandparents lived there as well. My family always took trips there. Although my sister and I didn't like going back to visit, we always were happy to see everyone once we got there. It was just my sister and I. We grew up in Alabama, and we hated it. It was too far, and it seemed like thousands of miles from Philadelphia. It took roughly about eighteen to nineteen hours to travel there by car.

My grandparents owned and lived on fifty-plus acres of land. Three houses stood on this land, all owned by my family. A dirt road led to and from our property. The other inhabitants of the land were cows, mules, bulls, dogs, chickens, and even snakes. My grandparents resided in the first house on the land, which was secluded except for one or two houses in view.

Big Momma, that's what we called her since she was my mom's aunt, lived in neighboring Dale County but still in Alabama. Many of the events that you'll read about occurred at Big Momma's house. She lived about forty-five minutes away, also in a very secluded area. The only thing in view from her house was the family church and a graveyard located across a very busy highway.

I remember tellig Big Momma that I didn't like coming to her house.

I assumed she knew exactly what I was referring to because she sharply replied, "They won't hurt you." It was a little while later when I found out that my mom and aunts didn't like going there either, due to some of the things they had experienced. The trips to Alabama just weren't good. I was convinced.

Acknowledgments

I'D LIKE TO THANK ALL THE people who helped me create this book and were very supportive.

My parents, Fish and Baybay, thank you.

Kid, thank you.

My kids—Rough, Ricky, Tinkerbelle, Buck, and CJ—thank you.

My sister, Lamoya Love, thank you.

My typists: Lieutenant, Thumbs, Mark, and Nef

Lieutenant, and Mark gave me the vision for how to put together this book.

Thumbs and Nef assisted me with typing this book. Thank you for all your ideas and dedicated time.

Carter, Taylor, Allen, Nina and few Other helped me with the name of this book.

I really appreciate you all. Thank you for everything!

Introduction

WHEN WE REFLECT ON OUR LIVES, there are pivotal experiences we keep in our memory. Some are good, some are bad, but there is something about each experience that sticks in our memory banks as if the memory happened yesterday. We all have these memories, and in some strange way, we store these images in our minds and catalog the emotions. This journey started when I was about five years old and continues to the present day. Most of my experiences were shared with other people in my family. I realize now the importance of sharing these events so other people can relate, learn, and grow from mutual experiences.

As I began to write this work, I shared the many episodes with my family. Some we laughed about, and others we hope we never go through again, but the unanimous consent was that everyone, to this day, still could remember each event. We all had/ have a different perspective, but despite our many views, many questions remain the same, such as were these spirits good and did they intend to do harm? These questions will be left up to you. My goal is to share what I have lived with my entire life. My hope is that as I present these experiences, we might learn.

Inspired by True Events

Shall we begin?

MY CHILDHOOD HAD AN INTERESTING TWIST. When I was growing up, my parents lived in a funeral home. My mother and father told me many stories about how I carried on as a young child. My father was an undertaker/embalmer, and my mother helped dress the body for presentation at wakes and private viewings. My parents told me that as a child, my playground was the twilight for the deceased. My hiding places were caskets, my towers where their tops, and my comfortable pillows were the insides—yes, those wonderfully cool, satiny inside Some of the memories are faint, but I think it gave me an unusual perspective when it comes to the dead. I was not afraid. To this day my mother reminds me that I would get frustrated when my playtime was interrupted by the arrival of family and friends of the deceased who were coming to pay their last respects and mourn the loss.

There is so much truth in the saying "What a difference a day makes." I can remember when my awareness changed from a carefree to an uncomfortable feeling. I was heading to the basement to get in my favorite hiding spot. I can't remember much about the day, but I do know that something changed. I nestled in the softness of the pillow for just a few moments. Suddenly a tingling feeling came over me. I didn't know what it was and could not describe it later when my mom asked me about it. I felt a coolness that soon turned so cold that I could almost smell it in the air. Even colder, my entire body responded in concert to this unique feeling. My heartbeat quickened, my jaws tingled, my spine tightened, and goose bumps ran along my arms and the back of my neck. My body's response in this way has been the staple of my fear throughout my life. I assumed that once I escaped this confinement all would be well. I never realized that the same feeling would stay with me into my adult life. My childhood fortress of safety became a dungeon that felt cold and uncomfortable.

The imprint sketched into my psyche remains in place today. I started to feel light touches and brushes against the hairs on my arms and legs. It was strange because I knew that no one was touching me, but I could feel my body react as if someone was close enough to touch the hair on my body without touching my skin. I desperately grasped at rational explanations since I was alone. That feeling of closeness was surreal, having someone barely touch my skin but be close enough to disturb the hairs. While I could neither see nor hear anything, I was certain that I was no longer alone. Uncertain about what I had just experienced, my pace quickened as I neared the top step from the basement. One thing is for sure: I did not turn around no matter how much I wanted to do so.

My mom was in the kitchen taking food out of the oven by the time I reached the safety of her presence. The roaster did not make it to the stovetop before I grabbed her tightly. A thinner woman would not have been able to catch her balance in time to save my father's dinner. I had a difficult time explaining what had taken place downstairs. Mom listened, although not attentively, as I explained the best I could. My ramblings were cut off as she reacted to the sound of Dad's car door shutting. Her attention returned to me once his plate was set and he settled in for dinner. She told me not to worry. "Everything will be all right," she said. If only she could physically see the tightening of my spine, no words would be necessary.

It had been weeks before I finally gathered the nerve to return to the basement. Mom told me that I would constantly complain every time I went downstairs. Each time I returned with a detailed account of something bothering me. At first, I'd walk out of the basement, but as time went on, I was running out. Eventually my mother banned me from going into the basement all together. So it was a surprise to my mother when I started getting the same feelings in other locations of the house. No longer was the kitchen an event-free area. Soon, my spine tightened when I was in the kitchen or the bathroom, or when I walked past the basement door, and eventually it didn't matter where I was in the house (funeral home). My spine tightening was frequent, uncomfortable, and unwelcome.

My sister and I

MY SISTER LAMOYA AND I ARE one year apart. I took after my dad while my sister took after my mom in looks and personalities.

My sister and I played during the day and spent a lot of time together. We'd have doll days, when we spent hours dressing our dolls and combing their hair. I remember one night Mom telling us to get ready for bed. Our bedtime routine was as predictable as the setting of the sun. She would prepare our bathwater, and we would giggle as we took off our clothes, run into the bathroom, and jump in the tub—and then wait for our scolding for running indoors. After bathing, Mom gathered our night clothes from under the pillow, which sent us racing off once again to see who could get dressed quicker. Our giggling in bed seemed to exhaust us to the point of falling into a deep sleep. Neither my sister nor I were the type of child who got up in the middle of the night. This night, however, was different as I recall my memories; this night was the pivotal night that began my visitations.

I woke up and tried to adjust my vision as I nudged my sister awake. We exchanged glances for a long moment. I was certain that she was seeing what I saw only because her grip on my arm tightened as she moved closer to me. Floating near the window was a lady with a white glow around her. There was no movement on her part at first, so we just stared clinging to each other. Our resolve dissipated once she drew nearer to us. Utter fear would be an understatement. The African American woman had shoulder-length hair, unfamiliar clothing, and that emanating white light all around her. Although she never spoke or gestured to us, her presence alone left a lifetime impression on me. As we began to break free from the bewilderment of fear, we gathered ourselves into a collective frenzy of screams. Our lungs held more air than either of my parents ever could have expected. The first note in our major concerto did what we had hoped because both parents hastened through the doorway, collecting each of us in their arms. Neither of us remembers the exact order of events, but we do agree that when we opened our eyes, the lady was gone.

It didn't take long for the questioning to start once Mom was assured of our physical well-being. Like floodgates giving way to the pressure, we let loose with all the emotion and tears that our little frames could muster up as we reported the details of the experience.

The two of us begged and pleaded to sleep the night away in our parents' room. Mom was about to give in until Dad gave her a look. We knew that look all too well.

It normally preceded a lot of grunting. To get us to calm down and return to the safety of our covers, Mom told us that it was probably our grandmother looking in on us. The thought did bring about a quiet sense of comfort. We were more comforted by the fact that we knew our parents would be up long after we drifted asleep again.

Lamoya and I laugh now about how fast our mom and dad descended into our room.

Let's go ... now!

IN THE COOL OF THE EVENING, every creak of a plank or rusty swing brings back memories of happier times. Not that my childhood was filled with sadness or pain, but I guess every child has his or her share. One evening, I sat with my mom and her sisters as they shared their individual accounts of the same stories. The stories were familiar and even more enjoyable each time I heard them. My mother's sisters, who were my treasure chest, held the family honors as well as its secrets. I remember everyone having a great time, and the mood was high. I hated that it was getting late because this meant I would soon have to retreat into the house and get ready for bed. Why did things always seem to get more interesting as the sun raced across the sky? Well, this time my hopes for enjoying more of the cool breeze and tall tales (or so I assumed) were dashed when one of my aunts suddenly got up and strangely suggested that everyone go into house with her at once. No one moved or even had a desire to go in the house, but she became even more persistent as she increased her pace toward the door.

I remember her words clearly. "If you could see what I see, you would get up and follow me through this door very quickly." As they all looked up, tracing the path of her last stare, resolve and confusion dissipated because in full view was a man crossing the highway, headless. I don't know why my mom took a moment to look away to see if the leaves were still yielding to the gentle breeze. Convinced that time had not stopped, and she was seeing along with everyone else what was real and heading toward them, her mouth flew open at the sight of this man getting closer at a steady pace. Everyone jumped up without uttering a single word or confirming what each of them must have doubted. As the adults peered out the door in amazement, the figure simply faded away. Well, at least that's what I heard as I nestled in the security of Big Momma's chair. Considering they all witnessed the same unbelievable occurrence, I thought all routines would be dismissed or overlooked. I really should have known that I would not be so lucky. I was marched off to prepare for bed. I overheard my mom on the phone telling my dad about the event. She told him that later that night she and her sisters started seeing shadows as they lay in the huge bed. Apparently, my aunt, who was on the end of the bed, felt something trying to snatch her out of the bed. She asked each of her sisters to switch places with her, and they told her no.

I didn't hear the rest of the conversation to bed.

For months and years, I wanted to know the rest of that story. I began to wonder what else she was shielding me from knowing.

My grandparents live in the South we had to go there every year for vocation and I was reminded of the luxuries I left behind.

Big Momma's house

SOME OF MY MEMORIES ARE FILLED with enjoyment and time spent with Big Momma, Grandma, and my mom. The conversations were very enriching for a little girl. I must say I learned a lot from the experiences. Now back to my harsh reminder that I was no longer in the city.

In the South, specifically Alabama, many homes did not have indoor bathrooms. Plumbing in most southern homes did not take place until homes were built or replaced during the late forties (1947). Depending on the time, location, and of course finances, the homes may have had an outhouse or a bucket. The outhouse was like a small closet. At Big Momma's, they used a bucket all day, and the bucket would later be dumped into a deep well about a hundred yards from the house.

I hated this aspect of Big Momma's house and would purposely avoid eating or drinking heavily because I didn't like having to relieve myself late at night. The thought of leaving the comfort and security of my covers was more than I wanted to deal with, but my body would betray me as it had done so many times in the past. Even though there was a calm about the night, it was the feeling of what could be there waiting in the darkness that always made me uneasy. One time I went to bed having had a full day and was ready to lose myself in unconsciousness. I got up and headed for the door of my room. The house was quiet, too quiet I thought, for this time of night—especially at Big Momma's house! I softly walked down the hall and then the stairs. As I walked,

I wondered where the pesky crickets were. That sound drove me crazy. Now that I wanted to hear the chirp to know I was not up alone, there was no chirp song to be heard. At the bottom of the staircase, I had to go left into the living room and then right into the kitchen or straight to exit the front door.

As I hit the bottom stair, I peered out the glass panel on the front door to see if the moon was bright. I saw the moon as my friend because it lit my path and gave me a sense of security. The night seemed less scary when my friend was shining bright. I smiled, jumping off the last step, but before I reached the ground, my calm was replaced by fright. In midair, out the corner of my eye, I saw something. To my right was a woman standing calmly in the kitchen next to the table and cutting a piece of cake. I froze as I watched this trespassing woman. I saw her holding a knife and the slice of cake tilt and fall as she motioned downward. Still frozen, I could not go forward or retreat to the security of my sheets. I'm thankful that everything froze, including my urgent need to relieve myself. I felt as though I were standing in hardened cement.

As the cake fell, the woman grabbed a piece, and looked up at me and smiled. When she saw me standing there. At this point the stranger looked directly at me. As her gaze caught mine, a sudden feeling of fight or flight took hold of me. I tried even harder to move, and in these moments of struggle, I could see her smiling at me even more. Unable to move or utter a sound, I continued my struggle. All I wanted was the security of my covers or Mom's arms. More exhausted than defeated, I closed my eyes, sealing them shut. For what seemed like a brief eternity, I stood there wondering, shivering, and crying within. The tap on my shoulder broke me free from the trance, but the experience was harder to escape.

My eyes shot open to catch the full view of Mom and Big Momma. Mom frantically tapped me on my shoulder, and Big Momma demanded that I answer her repeated question, "What's wrong, girl?" I saw them, but it was not until I was able to hear the familiarity of Big Momma's voice that I could move and speak. The lady was gone. It was no real surprise to me, though. In a mumbled voice, I began telling Mom that I was fine and explained what I had experienced. After I finished giving my account of what had happened, I realized I still needed to relieve myself. Big Momma and Mom accompanied me outside as I took care of my personal, private business.

I remember Mom trying to figure out who it might have been. She and Big Momma were calm and reserved as they exchanged ideas about who could have been in the house—in fact, not just in the house, but calmly standing in the kitchen cutting a piece of cake. Big Momma did not seem to get agitated until she thought about someone cutting into her cake. I was quite bothered by their relaxed state considering I was recovering from a traumatic experience. A little annoyed, I ran upstairs to the security of my covers. I overheard Mom say, "Ma, that red velvet cake is pretty good. I'm not mad at whoever it was 'cause that cake is good." Big Momma smiled and went to her room but not before I could barely hear her reply, "I been making that cake ever since I got the recipe from Sister Dale. Now that was a cooking woman. I sure do miss her."

It amazes me even today just how accepting my mom and Big Momma had been about the strange occurrences. I believe that was a turning point for me. After that evening, I never again wanted to return to Big Momma's house. Our family home for me was no longer a place of serenity, security, or carefree lounging.

let me go

I'M NOT CERTAIN WHY MY MEMORIES about Alabama are so clear. I experienced a lot at an early age. I can still recall being outside with my cousin Virginia and my sister, Lamoya. As I think back, I hate the fact that thirst interrupted my play and enjoyment. My mom asked me to go into the house to get some sodas. I was irritated that I was the one selected to do it, although my meddlesome sister was the one who initially asked for the refreshment. Well, thinking back, I guess it was more appropriate for me to get them since I was the oldest.

The house had double doors, but only one door was being used. The second door opened with a slap as if someone kicked it open and ran through. As I was getting the sodas, something took hold of me and would not let go. This feeling was very strong, and whatever it was had the tightest hold on me.

Fear welled up in me, causing me to recall the all-too-familiar feelings that had plagued me for years. The uneasiness and fright caused my spine to tighten. Overwhelming warmth encompassed my entire body. I became increasingly uncomfortable as my spine endured the pressure. No matter what I did or how I shifted, I could not shake the grip of whatever it was that held me captive. I saw nothing on me and yet felt clammy all over. I could not move or share my distress with my mom, who was only yards away but understandably distracted by my sister and cousin. At the point of sheer exhaustion, and after all my resolve had left, I was set free. I fell into the house instead of walking or running through the doors. My mom turned and looked at me as if I was crazy when she heard me hitting the floor. She asked me what was wrong, and I told her nothing, still confused and distraught from what I had just endured. She said it was time for bed and put us to bed. I just lay in bed thinking about the day's events. As I rose the following morning, I wondered if I had imagined the whole thing. It wasn't until later that evening when my sister asked me why I was playing on the porch behind Mom's back that I realized the experience was not only real, but it had been witnessed.

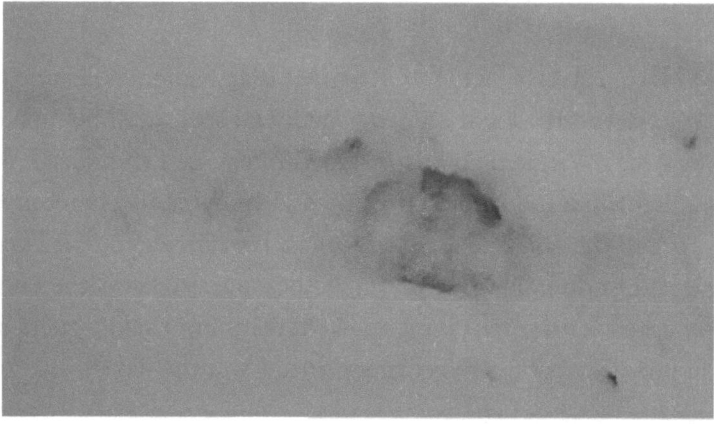

Is DAD my Protector?

MY FATHER WAS AN AWESOME AND multitalented man. I loved to hear him sing. He had a tenor voice, but then again I could be biased. On one of our trips to Alabama, I sat with Dad in Big Momma's living room and listened as he played the piano. Watching him tickle the keys and push the pedals gave me a sense of pride that only served to reinforce my image of him. He played softly for a moment and then seemed to make that piano sing on its own. It was a special treat to hear my father and sing together. He sounded wonderful with his group, but the music that he made with my aunts and uncles would have launched a great career if they were born at another time or in a different social situation. I wondered why nothing seemed to happen when Dad was around. It had only taken place when the womenfolk were alone. This realization gave me a renewed sense of comfort in the home that I no longer viewed as comforting or safe. But one day, shortly after Dad finished playing the piano, he closed the top and put the seat back under the piano. He and I were in the kitchen drinking and laughing. Out of nowhere came a tune that sounded very familiar. Scared, I moved closer and grazed my dad's arm while my spine began to constrict as it did when unwelcome experiences occurred.

My dad watched my frozen stare before acknowledging the sound. The tune also was familiar to him, and the source was unmistakable. Dad glanced at me once more, seeming to rationalize something. He turned after reassuring himself that he knows it wasn't me because I was with him. Dad reached the room's entrance before I did, so only he knew who or what had lifted the piano lid and pulled the bench out once more. I saw him, out of confusion and frustration, close the lid and return the bench under the piano. Would it remain there this time? I entered my summer bedroom and fell on top of my covers. I was highly frustrated and deeply disappointed that my dad was not able to keep the frights from tightening my spine. I couldn't believe that no one was able to keep me safe. Why?

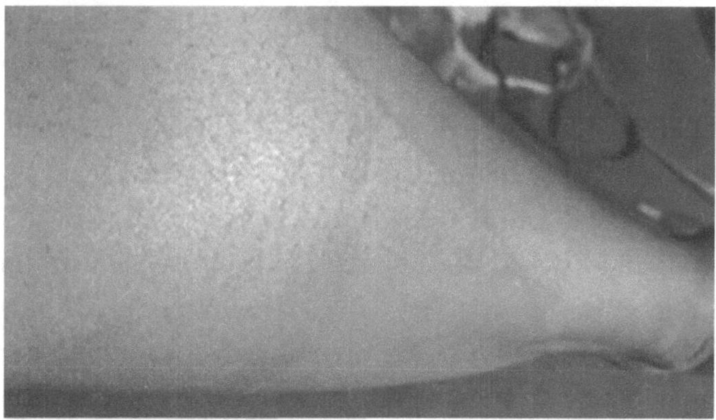

The chair at Big Momma's house

THE NEXT MORNING, MY GREAT-GRAND MOTHER was picking apples, and I decided to go into her house. When she walked by the entrance, there was a rocking chair that started to rock on its own. When she saw the chair moving, I went to the screen door and called for my cousin in fear. But she didn't come right away, so I headed to the kitchen to get a knife. On my way I heard the screen door open and close. Once I got the knife, I headed out the door, and as I was going out, the chair was still rocking. I was so scared because the chair had never stopped as long as I was in the house. I vowed to never return to that house, but I had to go back; I didn't have a choice.

So much had occurred to and around me during my trips to Alabama that I could hardly breathe or find enjoyment in the familiar smells and cool breezes that once ushered in the most wonderful memories. My southern experiences were becoming more than I could bear. I was walking through a thrift store one day, and I caught sight of a chair, a worn chair. There was nothing special about the chair except it reminded me of my great-grandmother. Big Momma's mother was special to me. I enjoyed her food, hugs, and belief in me. Her favorite chair brought me fear not comfort over the years. I believed sitting in that chair were dead people my grandmother had known. When she passed away, we had to go back there. Her scent permeated the air, reminding me of her unique smell. However, it was not the smell of old age but that of wisdom.

Thinking about her, I recalled the sad day that my world crashed, leaving me severely wounded. I sat in that old chair, and strangely enough I was comforted. All the love she had lavished on me through the years met up with me in that chair. Life gave me a moment to breathe again. As I sat there exhaling for the first time in what seemed like years, two distinct memories flooded my brain.

Shadow in the Night

EVERYONE HAD GATHERED AT MY GREAT-GRANDMOTHER'S house; she was still alive then. She lived across the walk from her daughter, Big Momma. One night I was awakened to another vision. I was so scared and felt my spine tightening. My kneejerk reaction was to scream, but I held my composure. I opened my eyes to see a clear shadow of a woman walking and holding a lantern. I could faintly make out what she was saying. Once I realized that she was calling my name, I retreated to the safety of my covers. I threw the covers over my head as a sure sign that I was scared to death. I closed my eyes and reached out for my cousin. At the very least I was not alone. My cousin and my sister saw the same thing I did, and they put the covers over their heads and started praying.

A yell finally escaped my lips. I heard myself yelling, "Oh Lord, she's calling my name." I must have awakened everybody, including my parents, because as I turned and looked, my parents were sitting straight up in their beds, eyes and mouths wide open. It was apparent they were seeing what I was seeing, and it was also apparent that they too were scared to death. After a while I was able to calm down. Will my nightmare now end? I wondered as I drifted off to sleep. Since my mind was a little clearer and refreshed the next morning, I was able to fully tell my mom what had happened the night before.

Chair Again

I WAS OUT BACK PICKING APPLES and enjoying the large yard. I was about to go back inside when I noticed the rocking chair that sat by the front door was rocking; then it stopped. There was no back door; therefore, I could clearly see the chair from the front porch. I must have been staring too long because the chair started rocking on its own again. Not again, I thought. I could not go back and tell my mom; she still would have made me go back. I barely made it inside the door, and the rocking increased. Not sure why, but I continued into the room and walked over to the screened front door, intending to call out to my cousin Virginia. But hearing the screen door open and close was not easy to take. Against my better judgment, I turned back, bracing myself for almost anything. I couldn't believe it. I didn't want to believe it, but it was true: the chair had stopped. The damn chair had stopped rocking. Not sure what to make of it, I continued for a few more steps, and I had the overwhelming desire to turn again. My body turned slightly, but I quickly decided against it, flew out the door, and did not stop until I got to my mom and told her I wanted to go home so I could feel safe.

I will never ever be going in that house again. It was sold to the state of Alabama, and both houses are gone for good. I know the spirits are not gone; they are still walking the grounds.

This is Forest Heights

MY FAMILY AND I MOVED TO Forest Heights in the 1980s. Our house were located behind a graveyard. The house was blue on the outside, and it had a huge backyard. Its consisted of a kitchen, a bathroom, a living room, and two midsized bedrooms. There was also a very small room like a den. We lived there for about five or six years. I should have known that something wasn't right with this house because of its appearance and the strange feelings I got when I just stepped into the yard. It didn't take long for things to start to occur in this house.

One night, coming back from a night out, my sister and I were sitting in the living room and watching TV. I could hear the silverware drawer rattling as if somebody was looking for something, and I also heard something running up the steps. The pots' rattling also sounded as if someone was looking for something. I knew by now what was wrong because I had that same feeling of the tightness of my back, which I usually got when strange, unexplainable things began to happen and grow by the second. So we ran out and waited for my mother to come home. My mother smiled and brushed off our testimony when she arrived. When I reflect on the experiences in that house, I always remember that I often heard children playing with what sounded like marbles in the hallways. At times you could even hear "imaginary" little girls running up and down the stairs in our home.

One day I heard the girls playing as my sister and I were watching TV. I acted as if I didn't hear them to see if my sister would say she heard something. When she did acknowledge the sounds, I was quick to comment on how I had been saying all along that I was not making up the stories about hearing these little girls.

As the noises got louder, my sister and I bolted toward the door and ran smack into our father. I started to tell him about the kids playing marbles on the steps, that they were very loud with all their laughter, and that there seemed to be a lot of children. I also told him about the two children's voices I heard the most. My dad smiled and told us to come inside. I told him about the time a little girl appeared and said this was their favorite spot to play and stated in her sinister little voice, "This is my house." I remembered when the girl said this, I was terrified, trembling. It was the way she said it and the mean look on her face and the fact that she was coming closer and closer to me. I thought she was going to attack me. I can't express the amount of terror I felt at that moment. Then she disappeared into thin air just as she had appeared.

Now do you Believe Me?

ABOUT TWO MONTHS LATER, I HAD an experience one night that woke me up. I wasn't afraid by this time because of all the things that had happened to me. My bed started shaking, which happened repeatedly and mostly at night. It felt like someone or several people rocking a car. One day my play sister, COOKIE , and I were talking, and I told her that the bed would shake at different times. She, of course, didn't believe what I was telling her. So one night my my play sister, COOKIE and I decided to sleep in the same bed, and it started moving. We woke up, and my sister was noticeably shaken by the experience. The look of terror on her face was kind of humorous considering she had never believed what I told her about this experience. Still half-asleep, I said, "You should have believed me. I told you the bed moved." And just like it usually did, the shaking eventually stopped. Still upset, my play sister, COOKIE, began looking under the bed, wondering what or who was causing the moving bed. As I figured, she didn't find anything.

The experience was so moving that to this day I can still remember and clearly describe how the bed moved. And one thing is for sure: the experience was so moving that my sister still talks about it. After we both calmed down, Lamoya looked at me as if for security. I nodded, and we lay back down and drifted off to sleep. That experience changed my life and my sleeping arrangements, as it did hers, from that night forward.

Lady

ANOTHER PUZZLING INCIDENT THAT TOOK PLACE at my Forest Heights home occurred while I was lying in bed. A lady wearing a white gown, who appeared to be African American, came through the door, looked at me, and smiled. Then she left through the window. What was unique about this experience was this woman was noticeably unattractive, but her facial features were well defined. She looked like someone with a pushed-in nose and no similar to a human form and the face of a bulldog. I was so scared I was screaming for my mother. She and my sister ran into my room, and I said to them, "This ugly lady just came through my door." I am not sure who this woman was; I had never seen her before. Maybe she had lived in the house or used to visit someone there. But with her assuring look, it appeared she approved of me being there, which was my main concern. We moved and I never saw that face again.

New Beginnings.... I hoped!

IN 1987 I GOT MARRIED. KID and I purchased our first home in Centerville, Pennsylvania. I wasn't a fan of the house. We went to look at it at night. I had bad feelings about this house like those of the past. But unlike the others, this was more of an eerie feeling. I told Kid I didn't like the house, but he loved it. I could not see why this house was scary. Outside and inside, the house was a little small for the family. But he couldn't see that and let the agent talk him into buying it. This was the first house we looked at, so we should have seen others.

An elderly lady had lived in the house for thirty years; she was in her late eighties. She sold this house and moved next door to her spiritual mother's house.

When we moved into this house, my parents moved with us. The house had two levels. The main level had three bedrooms, a living room, a kitchen/dining room, a bathroom, and a miscellaneous room with a washer and dryer. My parents moved back here from Florida. I had another bedroom upstairs that was an attic, suitable for living, and that's where my parents chose to settle till they move. The basement was cool and dark. To get there you had to go to the side of the house and down some stairs. One side of the basement had a dirt floor; the other side had a concrete floor. There were no walls except for the four that surrounded the basement. I was scared to go down there, but Kid occasionally had to because that's where the water pump and furnace were located. I never went into the basement and only peeked down there once from the steps.

One day Kid was in the basement, and he called for me to come down to see what he found hanging from the ceiling. There were jars with dead birds and rodents hanging in mason jars all over the ceiling. On the side with the dirt floor, there was a large stump and a mound of dirt that resembled a small child's grave.

Attic/Ceiling

THE SITTING ROOM OF OUR FIRST house had a drop ceiling. Only two rooms in the house had this type of ceiling. One of these rooms was the living room, and the other was the sitting room. Many times people, including me, would hear sounds coming from the attic while in the sitting room. On many occasions hearing these sounds were not limited to one person. There could be a group of people in the room, and the sounds would still come. The sounds were always the same, and they always came and went in the same direction. It sounded as if something was being dragged across the ceiling floor. I kept saying it sound like a very big snake. The sound was so penetrating and clear that anyone who heard it felt like whatever was being dragged could fall through the ceiling at any moment.

The disturbing feel about the sound was that it was slow moving and constant until it traveled from one end of the room to the other. It came at least two or three times a week—never at the same time but the duration was always the same. On occasion, if there were visitors, they would leave the room for fear that what was being dragged would probably fall. I often called animal control and similar companies, but upon investigation, they never found anything. When someone came to investigate, the process was always the same: the person would get a ladder, push up one of the panels, and use a flashlights to scan the area, but there were never any visual or audible signs of the noises. This went on for several months. As the sound traveled across the ceiling, the panels would flex and move as if something was walking or moving across the panels. While this was happening, no one ever popped up a panel to see if anything was there. The sound and movement of the panels were convincing enough that whatever was on the other side should stay on the other side. This was so constant that I even tried to get priests to come and bless the house. But the ceiling noises never left.

When I entered the house, many times I would peep around the entrance to see if the ceiling had caved in. The level of fear became so strong that I would not even go into the house unless someone was with me. After months of this, my father chose to end the madness one night. He decided to tear down the drop ceiling and close it up with standard drywall. As I look back now, my father's choice had a major effect on my life. As he began pulling down the panels, dust rolled off the tops of them. As the panels came down, the vastness of the ceiling began to appear as if it was the portal to another world. Determined to complete the job, my father worked through the heavy dust. As the panels were removed, he found dishes of all sizes and all types of silverware. Like the clutter of a child's room, these remains apparently were scattered over the various panels. When the entire ceiling was removed, I remember the moment my father made a startling discovery. He looked up high and said, "I'll be damned," as if he had just solved a puzzling mystery. My father found a door, very high above the attic, to what appeared to be another room. But he was determined to end the tyranny of the drop ceiling. Since there were no stairs to this room and know way to get to that room from the attic. I don't know how the things that was found that came out the ceiling could have gotten there, he opted to not investigate but create a permanent barrier by installing the new ceiling.

One evening I was in the house cleaning, and the children were out back playing. I started hearing and seeing little things as I cleaned. I could hear my father on the phone and music playing. I didn't think much of it and continued to clean. Then the phone rang, and the person calling asked to speak to my father. I started calling for him. I kept calling him and walked toward the upstairs bedroom. I never received an answer, and suddenly the music (that I thought I heard earlier) stopped. I checked the room and realized my father wasn't there. I went outside and asked the children if they had seen Granddad, and they stated that he was gone. I discussed this with my parents as soon as they got home. They told me that they had been experiencing some things upstairs from time to time, but they never told me because they knew I'd probably get scared. I told my dad that it was a lot of big and small holes in the front yard look like snake holes. He did see the holes, but he didn't understand how or why. But he told me it wasn't snake holes, I felt like it was something bad and it had something to do with that house. Nothing was good about that house I lived there in fear every day.

When my godchild, Sabrina, was little, she and some other kids came over for a sleepover one weekend, and she saw something. She hadn't been there an hour, yet she wanted to go home. I asked her why, and she just started crying. She was crying so hard that it hurt my feelings. Sabrina's crying got worse, so it started scaring the other kids. They wanted to go home, but they stayed. These spirits didn't care at all who saw them; they would come out of the walls at you. And that was terrifying. I feared my own house because I didn't know what was going to happen next. The house had a bad spirit.

Sabrina wouldn't stop crying because she was terrified. All she wanted was to go home, which was right down the street So I called her mother and told her that Sabrina was crying uncontrollably. Her mother met me halfway, and she told her mother that she saw something that scared her and wanted to go home. She wouldn't tell us what she saw. She no longer would stay at my house, and she also didn't want to visit. She never spoke of the incident again as a child or as an adult. She has gone to glory (July 2018).

Gone to Glory

THE PIVOTAL EFFECT OF MY FATHER installing the drywall ceiling was that it cost him his life. A week after my father completed it, he developed a severe lung infection. The doctors believed the dust was laced with a toxic chemical that coated his lungs, and two months later, after a week of hospitalization, my father passed away (November,1992). As I reflect on the sacrifice that he made, I often consider the price he paid to give me peace of mind. Many times, I blamed myself for causing my father's death. After the ceiling was installed, however, no one in the house ever heard that unique noise again, and I was truly grateful for what he decided to do. Who would have thought that it would come at such a painful, heartfelt cost?

Do you see what I see?

SHORTLY AFTER MY PARENTS MOVED OUT and into their own home, my older son moved into the attic. Not long after that he started having experiences as well. One night Buck and my oldest grandson were upstairs sleeping, and I was in my bedroom. The next thing I knew, I heard a lot of noise coming from the upstairs steps. buck burst through the door, out of breath, and with a look of fear in his eyes, he yelled, "Ma, where were you? I was calling you." I replied, "I didn't hear you." I honestly didn't. All he kept repeating to me was "I was calling you." He said something was holding him down, and he couldn't get up. No matter how hard he fought or how loud he screamed (or thought he was screaming), it wouldn't let him go. Over the next few days, all Buck did was pray through the house, and he told whoever or whatever that beast was that it would not run him or his family out of his home.

Later that Night

MY COUSIN LEON WAS IN MY youngest son's room. This was a very small room and had nothing but two windows, a closet, and a bunk bed. Ricky was on the top bunk, and Leon, who was over for the night, lay in the bottom bunk. We were discussing what had just happened with Buck, and the next thing I knew, Leon burst out of the bedroom door, screaming and hollering, with one leg in his pants leg while fiddling to get his other leg through the other pants leg. He stood there, out of breath, and said loud enough for the entire house to hear, "You all don't ever have to worry about me coming over here ever again." Minutes later I had to drive Leon home. He stayed true to his words and never returned to my house again!

On another evening, my son CJ and my daughter Rough were in the kitchen and decided to have some ice cream. As CJ was getting it out of the freezer, he obviously saw something because his mouth dropped open, and he dropped that ice cream and ran from the kitchen straight out the door without looking back or slowing down. When Rough turned around to see what changed CJ's mood, all she saw was a figure of what appeared to be a middle-aged woman in all white floating through the kitchen window. Rough stood there in disbelief and watched as the lady disappeared. Once she told me about what she saw, I realized that this was the same figure I occasionally saw as well. The kitchen was midsized, and there was a back door. At times you could hear someone walking around in there. My dad was usually asleep, and my mom was usually at work. The small hallway had white walls and a hardwood floor. Normally the first sound was of someone running up and down the steps. Shortly afterward, I would hear what sounded like marbles rolling across the ceiling (the floor of the attic).

32

Kitchen

ONE AFTERNOON I WAS WASHING DISHES in the kitchen. Ricky was playing on the floor. As I was doing the dishes, the cabinet doors flew open full force. As they swung open, all the dishes started flying out and crashing to the floor. My first reaction was to run. As I hit the stairs going out of the house, an empty feeling flooded my body. I realized that I was so petrified for the first time in a long time by this unexplained activity that I had left my son in the house and worse—in the kitchen. I ran back into the house and headed for the kitchen. Sitting on the floor with broken dishes everywhere was my son. He was crying and visibly shaken. I grabbed him up and ran back out the house. I waited for hours until someone came home so we could go back in together.

Kid got home first. We went into the house, and when I entered the kitchen, I noticed that the only dishes broken were those I used in place settings. In the South, many people set their kitchen table with plates, cups, saucers, silverware, and napkins, something you might see in a magazine like Better Homes and Gardens. I thought it was strange that even though the dishes were stacked in the cabinet with many other types of dishes, it was only selected dishes that were broken.

On several occasions I would hear from my children that they saw little girls or little boys. My son would see a little boy, and rough would see a little girl. I remember many times being in different rooms and feeling a breeze go by, almost as if someone was swatting something next to my ear. It felt like they were following me. Their presence was very noticeable as if they were violating my personal space.

One evening Kid and I were in our bedroom watching TV after dinner. The children were outside playing. Kid went to take a shower to prepare for work the following day. I called the children in so they could prepare for school the next day.

Later, after Kid and I had gone to bed, he woke me and shouted, "Go, go, go!" but as I looked around the room, I could not see what Kid was talking about. He kept hollering that a monster was coming out of the wall. Kid was so scared by whatever he saw that he crawled out from under the covers and headed for the light switch by the door. This was a pivotal moment for Kid because he had never experienced a clear view of such a scary, real-looking monster. When Kid turned on the switch, there was nothing there. As I told someone about this experience, I described the layout of the room. I explained that the light switch was close to the door. To the right of the bed was a window, and this window faced the front of the house. The person suggested that perhaps the monster needed the light to send to get rid of someone or something that was looking at the house from outside, and when the light came on, it sent whatever was lurking away in the dark.

"Do not go after those who make use of spirits, or wonder-workers; do not go in their ways or become unclean through them: I am the Lord your God.."

The Fight

IT WAS A SUNNY MORNING, AND I was getting the children ready for school. Kid had already left for work, so after breakfast I gathered the children and headed out to the car. Their school was about five minutes from home. I kissed and hugged the children goodbye and told them to have a good day. I watched them walk up to the school and pulled off once they were safely inside. I ran a couple of errands; I was gone for about an hour and a half. When I returned home, I heard what sounded like a serious rumble. As I approached the house, I could hear the noise coming from upstairs. It sounded like an all-out rumble. There were sounds of running, of a struggle, and of objects being thrown. It sounded like an all-out brawl.

I called a neighbor and asked her to go inside with me. The neighbor brought a black jack and I took the advice of my neighbor and got one of my German shepherds. Under normal circumstances the dogs would love to run in the house because they spent most of their time outside. But this day, when my dog Koko hit the third step of the stairs, she stopped (as if she saw something) and took off out of the house. The dog was so intent on getting out of the house that my neighbor and I had to go back outside and nearly drag Koko back in. When we finally got back in the house and went upstairs, everything was in place—almost as if nothing had happened.

One day, while in the basement, I was looking around and noticed what appeared to be a room behind a wall closet. Upon further investigation,

I realized that in fact there was an entire room behind the closet. This room was at least six feet square, and it had three concrete walls but was empty. Things were calm for a while, and we were beginning to believe that things had finally come to an end, or so we thought

China Cabinet

ONE EVENING AS MY DAUGHTERS AND I were sitting in the kitchen, we were startled by glass breaking in the china cabinet. This was a well-built cherry-oak cabinet. It had four shelves of thick, half-inch glass. Like most china cabinets, this one had the flat pegs that stick out of the wood it holds it in place. These pegs were solid brass with felt on the top. The glass shelves were perfectly made for the cabinet. They were not loose, and once in place there was no room for "foul play." So, once the top shelf shattered, the remaining shelves followed, imitating a house built of cards knocked down by the wind. That familiar feeling came. I remembered the tightening of my back … and moments later, I felt fine. I still remember the friend who gave me the dishes; she practiced some sort of nonreligious worship. This lady's personality was disingenuous. After you got to know her, you knew her talk and actions were insignificant. Once the dishes were destroyed, I never had that experience happen again. It was almost as if the dishes needed to be broken so what they represented was no longer part of the house. I wish this also meant that the things that happened in my home would cease and eventually end, but they didn't.

Things had been on the calm side once again, and we hadn't had any major problems. A few months later, Kid and I decided to sell our home and move into something bigger. Upon moving out, my mom and daughter Thumbs were doing one last walk-through of the house. My mom opened the attic door to make sure everything was done up there, and Thumbs was checking the bathroom to make sure it was empty. My son Ricky, our moving people, and I were outside waiting for my daughter Rough and Kid to come back from our new home with the truck so we could load up the last of our belongings and head out for good.

As we stood outside, we heard a bunch of rumbling and noises as if there was a fight going on in the house. It was similar to the rumbling noise I often heard upstairs. I then heard the attic door slam shut, and I remembered my mom and Thumbs, who was pregnant, were still in the house. I turned to enter the house, but before I could get my hand on the screen door, out they came screaming and running, almost knocking each other over. They were terrified. My mom's hair was standing straight up on top of her head. She was out of breath, trying to regain her composure, but worked up enough breath to tell me and everyone else standing there, "all these spirits never got to worry about me coming back to this motherfucker again." Just then my daughter Rough and Kid pulled up, and we packed up and left, never to return to that house again. Once we reflected on what had happened, we figured the spirits possibly did not want us to leave, or they were just giving us a scary, unforgettable goodbye!

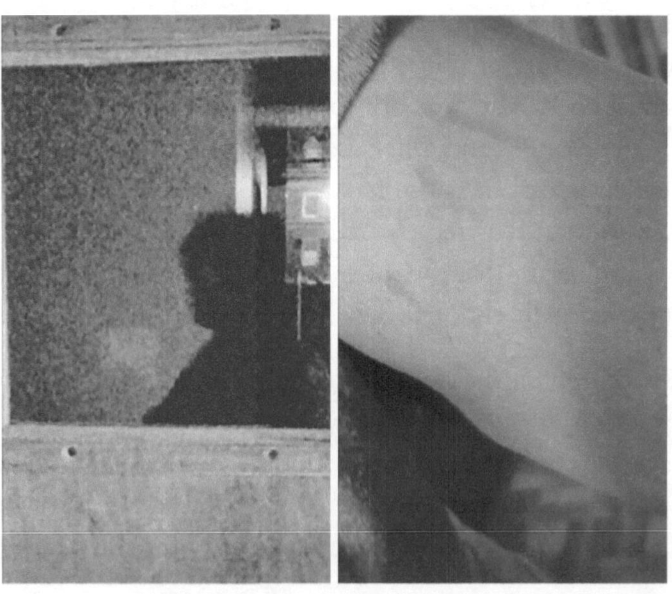

The Invitation

SHORTLY AFTER, KID AND I DECIDED to purchase a new home. As the search didn't seem long, we found one in Voltaire Heights, Pennsylvania. I liked this house a lot, and once again Kid fell in love with the house because it had a two-car garage with an upstairs. The house, which sat off the street, was made of brick and had white siding and a huge basement. The kitchen also was huge (just as I liked it), and there were two bathrooms, four bedrooms, a sitting room, and even a sunroom surrounded by windows. The house had hardwood floors, which I didn't care for especially because I had smaller grandchildren who often visited and a new baby coming in a few months. But that wasn't enough for me to say no to this home, so we purchased it.

After my family moved into the house, the visitations seemed to have gone away. A few weeks later, my daughter heard a knock at the door. I was in my room, so I didn't move at first. But after repeated knocks, I went to the door. Thumbs was the type who would look out the window to see who was at the door before she opened it. When she looked out the first two times, no one was there. The third time she looked out, there was a man who looked back at her but turned around. As he walked away, his figure faded away as well. This experience was unique because so many times she had heard this same knock but never found anyone at the door. On this day, even after spotting Thumbs and looking clearly in her direction as if to acknowledge her, he kept walking. Thumbs had the feeling that she was not the one he wanted to answer the door.

Days later, I was home relaxing and heard another knock at the door. I too did not respond immediately; there was a delay. But as the knock continued, I went to see who was at the door. When I looked out the window, I saw nothing. I paused but ignored the issue, thinking that maybe I was hearing things. As I walked away, the knock came again. This time I went back to the door, and for some reason, I felt I should open it and see if someone was outside. But when I opened the door, there was no one there. I looked in both directions, and to make sure, I even stepped out onto the porch but found no one. Thinking nothing of the incident, I went back into the house and returned to the bedroom. Kid was just coming out of the shower, and he asked lightly who was at the door. I replied that I didn't see anyone, but I wanted to make sure so I opened the door, but saw no one. Kid drew a blank look and seemed to be in deep thought. He later mentioned that whatever was outside could possibly now be inside.

I remember how angry Kid was, but as I reflected on the incident, a chilling thought ran through my body: No one before now had opened the door. But by opening the door, if something was there, it now had been invited inside because of my actions. My heart dropped, thinking that I could have been the very person to invite into our new house those same spirits that plagued the old house for years—or even worse, possibly different ones with God knows what kind of intentions. That night I kept thinking, what have I done? In the morning, I had hoped that I was wrong and that none of the old spirits where in the new home. My brother-in-law was in his room asleep, but something was on him, and he couldn't move or say anything. He was trying to get his feet on the floor and his hands on the wall to get it off of him, but it held him down. Finally it let him go. He was scared then, and he was cursing, He didn't know what was going on, but he knew the house was haunted.

As time went on, we did a tremendous amount of work to the new home. We got wall-to-wall carpet installed. We completely renovated the basement. One day I decided to do a little more cleaning but started having problems when the vacuum cleaner wouldn't work. It would come on and cut off. I borrowed a vacuum cleaner from my play mother, and that didn't work, either. So I took it back and told her it didn't work. She didn't believe me, so while I was at her house, I plugged it up, and it worked. We looked at each other and laughed, and I just said, "Well, thank you for letting me borrow it. Guess I have to try to purchase a new one and see what happens."

I bought another vacuum cleaner, and that one did the same thing. When I took that one back, the store checked it out and found nothing wrong with it. Unlike the last time, instead of just leaving it, I decided to take it back home and try again. It worked, and I had no more problems. I figured what it might have been and was secretly hoping this wasn't a result of uncertain experiences and why I'd had so many unexplainable complications with these vacuums. But I quickly dismissed the thought. I was just happy that my vacuum worked, and I could clean my home like I wanted to.

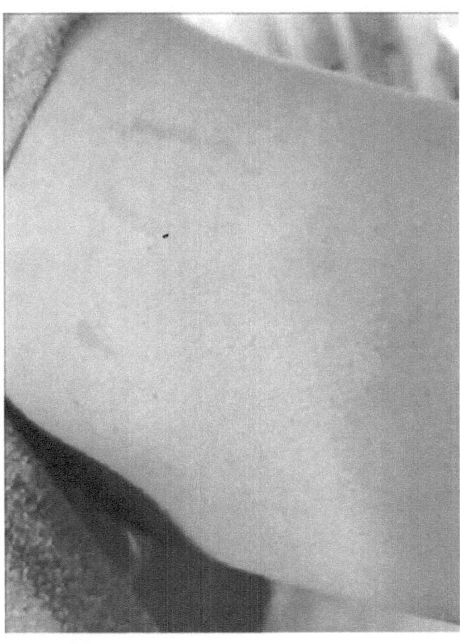

Sleepwalking

WEEKS LATER, IT WAS ONE OF the nights that my worries were confirmed. We had just gone to bed and must have dozed off while watching TV. I awoke to the sound of shuffling. I opened my eyes a little bit, enough to look around the room. I noticed that Kid, while appearing to be asleep, had gotten out of bed, stood there for a few minutes, and walked toward the door. He then turned around, facing me, and continued to stand and watch me for what seemed like minutes but was only seconds, He returned to his side of the bed and gazed in the direction of the TV.

I had been watching his actions, and as I began to speak, Kid got into bed. Within seconds he was peacefully in a deep sleep, as he returned to snoring. I reflected on the fact that just before I was about to say something to Kid, his body reacted as if he had been talked to—no words—just the thoughts in my mind. This was a new experience for me. I had been married for over twenty years, but I had never seen Kid respond and move in this manner.

Weeks later, a similar incident happened. It was late one night, and he was sleeping, but I was still watching TV. Suddenly Kid arose again. He got up, walked to the end of the bed, and gazed toward the window. I watched him to see what he was going to do. I watched for some time, and he was motionless. This time I began to call to him, softly at first, but he didn't move as if not there. I continued to call him, raising my voice. After several times Kid, who appeared to be awake, responded as if he was dazed and unaware of why he was standing. As Kid returned to bed, I asked him why he got up. His responses were sporadic as if his sleep had been interrupted. I asked additional questions, such as what had happened weeks earlier, and his response was that he was not aware of it even happening. What troubled me was the gaze on his face. I still describe it as if Kid was not in possession of his body. As we both settled back into our sleep, I reflected from that point on. I would now watch and wait to see Kid's actions as he got up in the middle of the night. To this day he has slept through the night most nights since this happened.

Family Time

WE WERE GETTING MORE AND MORE used to the home, despite the little mishaps that happened from time to time. We spent most days unpacking and adding finishing touches and designs to my liking. One night, my daughter's friends were over, and they were taking pictures. Just as we usually did when we took pictures of fun times, we gave them to Mary (a friend of the family) to process and print. She called and said we needed to see these pictures, so she brought them to the house. There was a man's shadow behind Rough in several pictures. In one picture, there was a man sitting on the other side, wearing a hat, and what looked like a child. I showed the pictures to several people to see if they recognized or saw what I saw. Yes, everyone we showed the photos to saw the same things. We were relieved that we weren't the only ones to see them. We put the pictures up for safe keeping and, if needed, future reference.

As time went on, I sometimes would see shadows. I would see a dark shadow go past very quickly. Sometimes it would be a big body or a small shadow or a dark ball. A picture in the kitchen would fall off the wall, and it was a big picture. When I went upstairs, I could feel a presence walking and hear sounds. I would look, and once I saw that nothing was there and that it must have been just a shadow, I would chalk it up as another unexplained experience.

No one was allowed to go into my living room, and we only got together there for special occasions like Christmas or if company was over for

Thanksgiving. It was very well decorated. There was a large mirror in the living room, and it would often fall off the wall. Again, this was a very big mirror and was attached to the wall securely. We would simply put the mirror back up and hope it wouldn't fall off again—and be thankful that it didn't break. The living room was connected to the stairs that led up to my son's bedroom. Often when I went upstairs, I could feel a presence behind or in front of me. Sometimes I could see a shadow (a figure of a man) in front of me. At first, I thought that I was the only one seeing it, but then my son asked me if I sometimes saw a shadow when I went upstairs. I replied, "Yes, you see it too?" He said, "Yeah, all the time." Relieved, I said to myself, "Thank God, I'm glad I am not the only one." I didn't and still don't like staying in the house alone because I always see things or hear things.

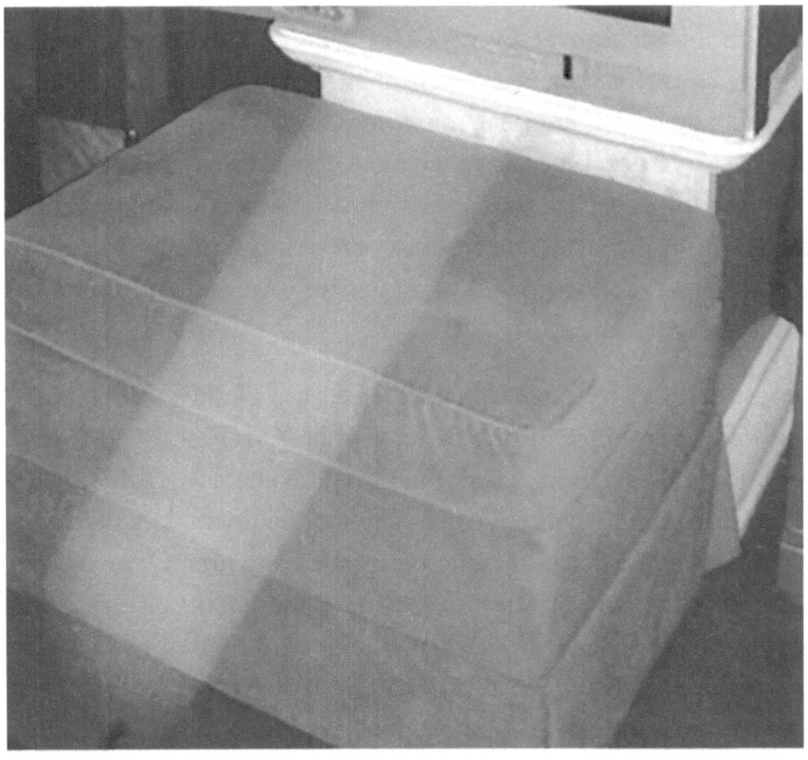

Blue

WHEN WE MOVED, WE BOUGHT OUR extended family member because that is exactly what we considered him—a family member—and we treated him as that. He was our small dog, Blue. I had him for a little over seven years. He didn't like to play upstairs at the new house for some reason; at times he would have a fit about not going up there. I know that sometimes dogs can see things that we can't see, so I knew Blue had to have experienced something by the way he was acting. Then he started getting sick. This was apparent due to changes in his behavior; for instance, he would start growling at Kid, our son Ricky, and me. He'd be aggressive toward us, snapping at us for no reason.

Because of the shift Rough worked and because Thumbs was bedridden, they were often home during the day while Kid, Ricky, and I were at work. It got to the point where Blue would come downstairs when we left for work and sit by Rough and Thumbs's bedroom door until one of us returned home that evening to be upstairs with him. One day Rough let him outside, and he ran into the street and got hit by a car. About two hours later Blue died. This was strange because Blue had never run into the street before. We always had let him out the front door and allowed him to roam freely throughout the huge yard. Although we lived on a main road, he knew to never go in the street, and he didn't—until that day! I always wondered what led Blue into the street. Or even worse, did the spirits lead Blue into the streets?

Blue was such a lovable, happy dog. For him to act like that and behave the way he started behaving was shocking. It had to be something haunting him upstairs.

A few months later we got a new dog named Smokey. He also spends most of his time upstairs like Blue did at one point.

Smokey

ONE EVENING, AS I WAS SITTING on my bed looking through some catalogs. Smokey jumped up on the bed, ears standing straight up. He was staring at the other side of the room where my closet was. He started making a whimpering sound as if he feared something in that direction. I looked up to see if I could see something, trying to understand what was going on. Smokey would not move; he didn't even want to get off the bed. This was unusual because Smokey had never acted this way before. He was a very playful puppy. At times, when in the room, he would be a little aggressive but normally only toward Kid. I do wonder from time to time, though. Does he or will he too experience strange things that Blue might have seen or experienced?

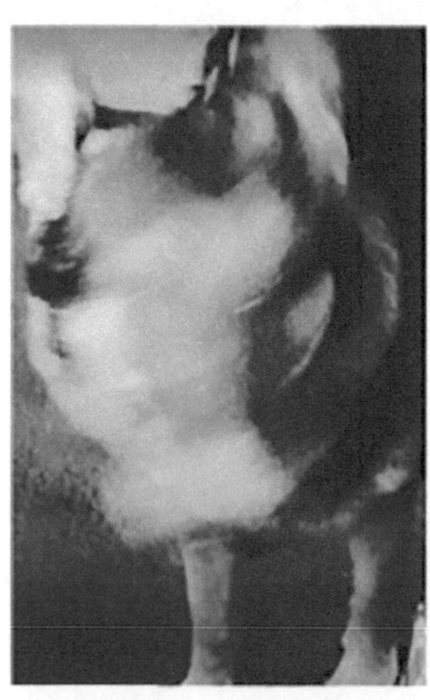

In the house

AT TIMES THE HEAT IN THE house would go up to ninety degrees. I would turn it down, and it would go back up. It was as if the thermostat worked when it wanted to work. If we would turn it off, we wouldn't be able to get it back on. When we were finally able to get on, it wouldn't turn off but repeat the same thing, which was turning up the heat and no one knew how. I asked everyone in the house, and Kid asked me and everyone else as well, if someone had turned up the heat. We got the same result every time: no one knew how the heat got turned up. One day when I was finally able to turn it off, I said forget it and left it off, and I told everyone not to touch it. It stayed off the entire winter, and we went without heat. I suggested that everyone purchase space heaters for their rooms because we were no longer interested in fooling with that thermostat. The following winter I tried it again, and the same thing began to happen, so before we could repeat that cycle, once I got it turned off, I left it off.

Sometimes there was a very strong, fruity scent like that of perfume in the house. You could often smell it. I was not much of a perfume wearer, but this scent was unlike any of the perfumes I owned, or that either one of my daughters owned. Another very strange scent was that of a cigar. This too was very strong sometimes, and no one in the house smoked cigars. Never mind the fact that this house was not adjacent to any other houses. It sat alone with nothing attached to it. So I knew this cigar smell couldn't possibly have come from a neighbor's house. The smell was so strong that it was as if someone in the house was smoking a cigar.

There were times it would be very cold in spots of the house—you suddenly felt cold and it got very chilly—but as soon as you would notice it and make note of it to others in the room, it would simply go away.

Sometimes you could feel a strong presence behind you, almost as if something was right behind you, only to turn and find that no one was there. I often felt something on my neck like a swipe of a soft touch, and no one or nothing would be behind me. One evening I was upstairs in my room. It was just Thumbs and I in the house. Thumbs called upstairs to tell me that she was about to go to her boss's house for a little bit. She was going to jump in the shower and asked me to listen for the baby, who was sleeping. After a few minutes, as I was going downstairs, I heard the microwave door close and the microwave turn on as if it were in use. Thumbs was coming out of the bathroom. She asked, "Mom, what are you fixing?" I was just hitting the bottom stairs and asked her, "So that wasn't you using the microwave?" She said, "No, I told you I was jumping in the shower!" I said for clarity, "So there is no one in the house besides us?" She laughed and said, "No, I thought you were fixing something."

We both went to the kitchen to check, and sure enough no one was home or had come in; we were still home alone. Frightened, Thumbs shook her head, went into her room, and continued to dress, and then she left. I was almost in disbelief as I told her to make sure she locked the door, and I went back upstairs. I was not sure I wanted to stay home alone, all by myself.

A few nights later, Thumbs was in the shower. This time it was just Thumbs, Kid, and I home at the time. As she was showering, the light turned off. She peeked out of the curtain, and the light popped back on. She resumed showering, and the light turned off again. She called out to see if maybe Rough or Ricky were playing with the lights because she was afraid of the dark, and they often played tricks on her to scare her and even make her cry. (As mean as it sounded, they still all laughed at the end of the joke.) When Thumbs got no answer, she washed quickly and immediately got out of the shower. The second time this happened to her, she again called out to see if they were playing a joke on her. When there was no answer, she nearly killed herself trying to get out of the shower. It seemed as if this had become a regular thing, for when Thumbs got into the shower, the light would go off and come back on—on its own! She was so shaken up from the experience, that it got to the point that she would shower with the bathroom door open, or sometimes not shower unless Rough was home (since they were both on the downstairs floor), or shower when everyone was home and moving around. By this time unexplainable things were really starting to happen and rapidly.

Shaking of the door

ONE EVENING KID WAS HOME ALONE, and he heard the door to the basement close. He got up to see if someone had come home, but he found no one. So he went back upstairs to resume watching television. A few moments later, something started shaking the bedroom door. He got up to see if someone had come in although he had just checked the house. Then he called me on the phone and said that something was shaking the bedroom door. I told him I'd never heard that before.

A few nights later, I was home, and everybody else was gone. I heard a little shaking of the doorknob. I thought, That must be what he is talking about. I thought nothing of it and went back to watching TV. About two days passed, and I was home alone again. This time the door started shaking a little harder than before. I didn't know what to do, but the door suddenly stopped shaking. I waited for a while, opened the door, and ran downstairs until someone came home. I called Kid and told him what was going on, and he replied, "I told you."

About a week later I was in bed, watching TV, and the door was closed. My son Ricky came in, said something to me, and left the room but didn't close the door. He came out the bathroom and was about to say something, and the door slammed in his face. Scared, he opened the door and said, "OK, Mom, you couldn't have closed the door; you're lying in bed." He came in the room with his father, but by this time I was asleep. The door was still open, but it closed on its own. I jumped up, and Ricky jumped on the bed next to me. Moments later, the door handle started shaking hard as if someone or something was trying to get in. Kid got up, and the door started up again. He got behind the door, but when he opened it, nothing was there. We all looked at each other in disbelief, each of us knowing deep down the cause of this wild experience. After we all calmed down and my son said good night, he went to his room, closed the door, and got into bed. Kid closed our door and got into bed as well.

That same night the door started up again, except this time it was worse than before. I put the covers over my head and started praying; Kid didn't know what to do. Ricky lay in his room thinking of all the things that had happened that evening. In the meantime, his door handle started shaking just like mine had earlier that night. He told me about it the next morning. I asked him, "What did you do? Did it just stop?" He said he threw the covers over his head and started reciting a prayer that I told him usually helped when I experienced these things, and it soon stopped. Unable to get back to sleep, Ricky just lay there reviewing the events of that evening. He said these thoughts kept him awake all night. What he didn't know was that I too was up all night the night before.

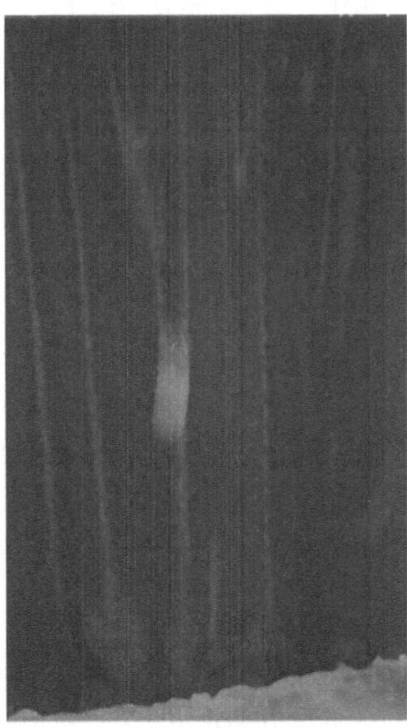

Closet!

MY BEDROOM HAD TWO CLOSETS, A big walk-in closet and a small one, similar to a hall coat closet. One morning, I saw a light on in the corner of the right-hand side of the big closet. I tried to look for the light, but after a few minutes of no luck, I said, "Forget it," as I was in a hurry. I thought nothing of it and headed out. I went downstairs to meet Kid, who was waiting to take me to work. For some reason, however, I still couldn't get that light off my mind and thought that I forgot to turn it off. Then it hit me: There was no light!

I stopped dead in my tracks, turned around, and headed back through the kitchen and up the stairs to see where that light was coming from. When I walked into my bedroom, the mysterious light was gone. Puzzled, I headed back downstairs and to the front door. Kid asked me what was wrong—I assumed he had seen the puzzled look on my face— and I told him nothing and proceeded out to the car. Unbeknownst to him, however, there was something wrong, very wrong, and I had to know what it was.

Beside my closet was a little square window. It faced the backyard of the house. At times I would see something going past the window, usually resembling a shadow, in very slow motion. Sometimes, if other family members were home and Kid and I were not there, they reportedly would hear something moving around upstairs in my bedroom where the closet was. Until this day I have never found that light, and I haven't seen it since then. It is still a mystery where it could have been coming from.

Although the spirits often scared us, we often believed that they were trying to wake us up so we wouldn't be late for work. If Thumbs or I might oversleep, they would do something to make us get up, such as whisper in our ear or slightly rock us. And when we'd wake up, we found no one there. One morning I was asleep, and the alarm clock was going off, as I often did, I shut it off and went back to sleep. Something whispered in my ear clear as day, "You'd better get up!" I jumped up and said okay, but once up I looked around and found no one in my room with me. After hurriedly getting ready for work and checking my children's rooms on my way out of the house, I found that there was also no one home but me!

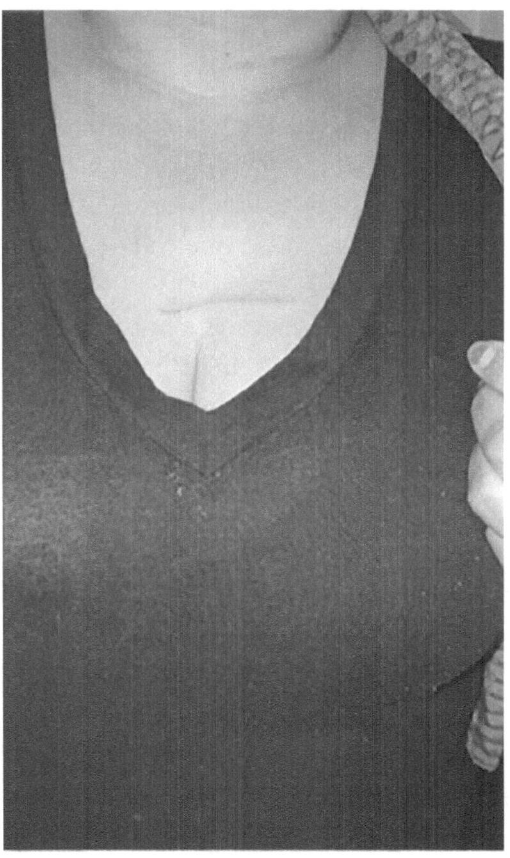

Mom Connie's House

I WAS OFF FROM WORK ONE day and home alone again. I was a little bored so I decided to try out this new casino game I had purchased. In order to play, you had to plug it into the TV using the red, yellow, and white cords. I was playing the game on the TV when it starts playing by itself. It looked as if something or someone was pushing the button down on the game. I turned off the game and put it away. Then I took the game over to my mom Connie's house, and the game started doing the same thing—it was playing by itself. Once I showed her this, she snatched the plugs out of the television, packed it up, and told me to take the game home and not to bring it back. We laughed, and I put the game in my trunk of my car and returned to mom Connie's house.

I went upstairs to the bedroom looking for something she told me to grab for her. Suddenly, I heard scratching behind the door as if someone/ something was trying to get my attention. I hurried out of there and back downstairs to her, and I told her what happened. Since I never got what I went for the first time, I went upstairs for a second time. As I was headed back downstairs, I began hearing things behind the door again, except this time it was in the other bedroom, and it was louder. This was the second time this happened, and apparently no one could hear it but me. I went back downstairs and told her it was happening again. She went to retrieve what she needed and returned without hearing a peep. At that point I was put out (with love). I never found out what that noise was or why I was the only one who heard it—or I was the only one whose attention the spirit was trying to get.

Work

ONE DAY I WAS AT WORK, and I had to make rounds. The first time I made rounds, I saw my shadow walking toward me—not to the side of me but in front of me. I didn't pay any attention to it at first, but as time went on that day, it happened again. So I kept doing my rounds, and the shadow came up again. I stopped; it stopped. I would move to the side, and it would do the same. I took off running to tell my coworker what was going on. It seemed like no one believed me at first, but each day something would happen. Then it would stop; I wouldn't see it anymore. About three days later, it started up all over again, and each time it got worst.

One time I was walking down the hall, and the shadow was coming toward me just as before. I was scared, but I just kept walking. The shadow stopped in front of me, and I figured if I stopped and looked, it would leave me alone. I did just that. I stopped, and I looked. As I looked from its feet up to its head, I realized the shadow didn't have a face. It was dressed as a security officer and was a replica of me, except one damn thing: it didn't have a face. I ran to the other side of the building and told my coworker. I never went back down there.

After a while I was moved to another department, and when I made my rounds, I could feel a presence. I didn't pay it any mind until I felt as if something was following me. I would hear things walking over my head and behind me, and I would get very cold. So one night I took another officer with me to the same place. He also didn't like it down there; he said it felt spooky. Whatever was down there touched me in my ear, almost playing in it. I told the officer, and he didn't believe me. I didn't like going to secluded parts of the building. I would always take someone with me when doing rounds.

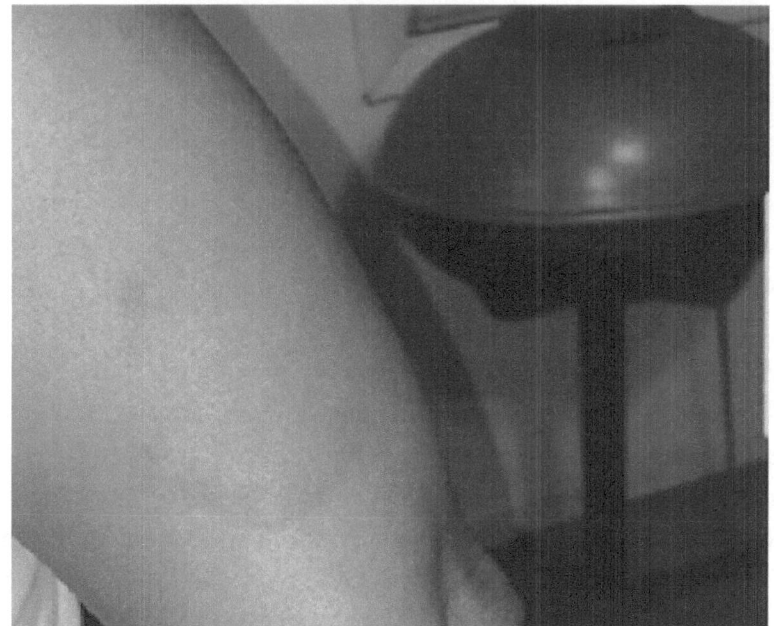

Moved out

A COUPLE OF YEARS LATER, THUMBS and Rough moved out to an apartment complex about ten minutes from me. We sometimes believe that the things followed them to their apartment. At times the water would come on in the bathroom and kitchen, but when Thumbs got up to check, the water would turn off. Glasses fell off the counter, once filled with water, and when Thumbs went to see what the disturbing noise was in the kitchen, she would find the glass sitting upright like someone simply sat it on the floor. Lights would go off and on by themselves.

One night Thumbs went to the store, and when she got there, she couldn't find her wallet; she knew she had taken the wallet with her. She looked everywhere in the car and couldn't find it. She decided to go back home thinking maybe she did leave her wallet there. After a thorough search, however, she saw that she had not left it there. She decided to check the car one last time, and when she got back to the car, the wallet was on the seat. She considered going back to the store since she had found her wallet but decided against it since because she was scared to drive alone, thinking that the sprits had gotten into the car and possibly followed her to the store.

Another time Thumbs was taking a shower, and when she got out, she went to get the deodorant. She had the deodorant in her hand and the phone rang, so she put it down on the toilet and left the bathroom to answer the phone. When she came back, the deodorant was gone. She knew where she had left it. She looked everywhere in the bathroom for it and then went to the living room where she went to answer the phone. Nothing. Thumbs went back to her bedroom and even checked the kitchen, but it wasn't there. When she returned to the bathroom, it was sitting on the toilet seat—exactly where she recalled leaving it in the first place. All that time the deodorant wasn't in the bathroom, and no one was home with her at the time. She didn't know how it got in the bathroom when it wasn't there the three times she checked. She was so scared because she thought maybe someone was in the house with her. Or maybe Rough had come home and was playing a trick on her.

Then the lights started going off and coming back on. Once again Thumbs was so scared that she didn't know what to do. She called me and told me what was going on, in the house she was so scare. She sat outside till someone came home. Thumbs was in the bedroom watching TV, and the light turned off. She got up to turn it back on, but it wouldn't turn on. She sat down, and the light came back on. Later that day, the TV went off, but this time Rough was home. Thumbs told her what had happened earlier with the light, and Rough, who was used to unexplainable things, smiled slightly and resumed watching TV. She knew exactly what was going on in their home.

Suitland Parkway

ONE MORNING I WAS ON MY way to work, and Kid was driving. I yelled,

"Watch out! Don't you see those people walking across the street?" He said he didn't see anything. I told him about ten people carrying things on their heads were crossing the street, and they looked like slaves. When I was in college, I had seen spirits at night trying to cross the street in different places and Suitland expressway was slaves.

Another time Kid was going to pick me up from work. This big, bright white something was flying in front of the car. I said, "Do you see that?" And he said, "Yes, what is it?" I didn't know; it flew away to the woods. I thought about it and said,

"I think that was my spiritual mother telling me she is okay."

In the room

I'M REMINDED OF A TIME WHEN I came home from work about midnight. I changed my clothes and went to my daughter's room and stood in her doorway talking to her. As I got off work late at night and my daughter was a night owl, we were often up late at night chatting, watching movies, and laughing at the never-ending crazy events we had experienced that day. This night Rough and Thumbs came to spend the night as they often did. Rough asked me if I wanted to watch a movie with her, and I said I would. We went to the kitchen to get something to snack on during the movie and went right back to her room. When we got back there, her refrigerator door was wide open, and we got scared because Thumbs was sound asleep in the bed—knocked out. Neither one of us had come in the room for anything until that moment when we entered together. Both of us knowingly looked at each other, shook our heads, shut the door, and watched the movie as planned.

Marks

THE FOLLOWING NIGHT MY LEFT ARM started to hurt, so I looked at it and saw that I had a long mark on it. I got cold. My daughter Rough was standing there, and I said to her, "It feels like something is standing right beside me." What happened was a mystery to me because I didn't feel anything at the time, and until this day it puzzles me. How did the mark get there? After I showed it to my daughter, we didn't know what to do, and at that same moment, we heard someone running down the steps. Everyone in the house was asleep except for us, but it happened three times. I was scared to go upstairs and get in the bed. So I waited, and the noises continued, Eventually I went upstairs, got into bed, and finally dozed off to sleep.

The next morning the noises started up again. My dog looked in the direction of the noises and got scared. He almost hung himself trying to get next to me. So I said, "Go away, leave us alone, go to the light. We don't want you here." I know when my dog can see them by his reactions; he moves frantically like something is bothering him. About two days later, I took a picture of my arm on my phone and then I was searching through the other photos when a lady appeared on the screen. The lady had a dark-skinned complexion and very long, wavy, dark hair. The picture was of her profile.

The next day I was trying to send the picture to my other daughter's phone, and instead it went to my sister in law phone. I was trying to show them what was on the picture of things happening in the house.

She called me and asked, "Who is this in the picture, or who was it?" I told her I didn't even know the picture went to her. She suggested that maybe the spirits were mad because they didn't like the idea of me talking to her and asking for help with removing them from my home.

All my experiences had never been what you might call harmful, but it's different now. It's like they're bothering me, almost trying to harm me and those around me. I've never felt uneasy before, but lately I have been. They've been around me all my life, but I've never feared them like I do now. Even my daughter, who normally isn't scared, gets a little scared now.

One night we were sitting in the TV room watching the movie Insidious. The movie ended, and I took it out of the DVD player. Suddenly the movie started playing again and the movie was on the table the player was empty. We decided to let the movie play I was to scare to try to stop the movie, not wanting to get them upset and didn't want to know what was next. The movie just played and eventually ended, so I got up to check the DVD player. Lord behold, there was the damn movie in the player and I know I took the movie out the player and put it on the table. I just took it out and put it on the TV In our TV room we didn't know what to do but I do know I will never look at that movie again.

We had a desk with a computer set up in the corner. They obviously liked the chair at the computer. Often it would go down as if someone had sat in it, but no one would be in the chair or, even worse, near it. Or the chair would swivel around although no one had touched it. The spirits even did things like take our personal belongings— our keys, cigarettes, etc. We would search all over for these items and find nothing; I mean I'd have no luck at all. Then a few days later we would find we thought we had left them originally, as if they were never touched and were there all along. Or they would be somewhere completely different from where we left them, even in places where we had looked previously and didn't find anything.

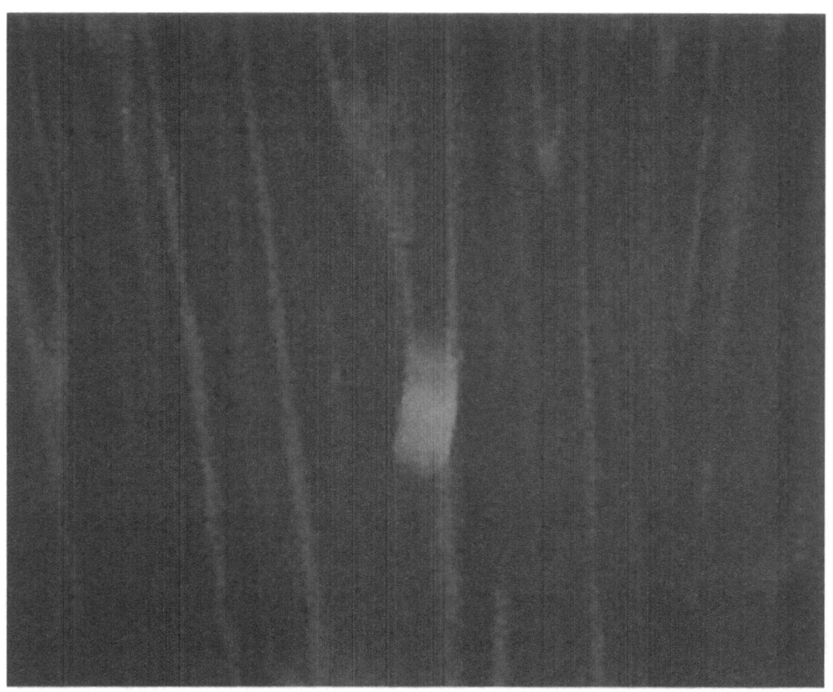

Keys

ONE EVENING BEFORE I LEFT FOR work, I placed my keys
on the dresser since Kid would be picking me up later that night, and
he often used my car. I received a call from Kid, and he asked me,
"Where did you put the keys?" I told him they were on the top of the
dresser, where I placed them every day. He called back stating that he
had searched all over the dresser, the room, and even other parts of the
house. Worried that he'd be late picking me up, he just drove his vehicle
instead. Once we got home, I joined in the continuing search for my
keys. Out of curiosity we began to check random places and even the
dresser drawers. Somehow they appeared on top of the dresser where
I recalled placing them earlier that day. We looked at each other in
disbelief, wondering how the hell those keys got there.

A day or two later I received a call from Rough, who said her keys were
missing. I had a spare key to her car, so I told her I'd be there shortly to
give it to her. I asked her if she was sure she had searched everywhere.
She said that she and Thumbs searched their entire apartment. They
often laid the keys near the door or on the entertainment center, but the
keys weren't there. So I gave her my spare and went home. Maybe two
days later I was at their apartment visiting. Thumbs was straightening
up, and she went to place something on the entertainment center—the
keys were lying right there. The only thing that Rough, Thumbs, and I
could do was sit/stand there in disbelief. This sent goose bumps down
Thumbs's arms. I just laughed on the inside wondering why the spirits
were playing with our keys.

Fear

IT'S TO THE POINT THAT I don't like to be alone in my house, especially in the basement. I always get a feeling of fear, and then it goes away. I went in the basement to wash my clothes, and I felt like something was down there, but I proceeded anyway. It got so cold that I tried to see my breath. The basement always had an eerie feeling as if something was down there.

Because of the strange things going on around the house, I decided to get the house blessed. When it was blessed, I was told that there were spirits downstairs in the basement and upstairs in Ricky's room and my room. The basement gives the same effect as some of the other areas in my house. We often just go down to wash clothes, do what we need to do quickly, and come back up.

Not Just Me

ON RICKY'S TWENTY-FIRST BIRTHDAY, HE WAS lying in bed. Something suddenly came over him, and he couldn't get up and out of the bed. He was trying to get up, but whatever was going on was holding him in place. He was screaming, but no one heard him. He couldn't move, so he started praying. This had never happened to him before, but he remembers me telling him about something similar happening to his older brother. He had only heard me talking about it. Both boys said it felt like a witch was riding them and holding them down. You can't move; you can't say anything. You try to say something, except no one can hear you even though they may be right next to you. When it's over, you are scared and don't know what happened. Then you ask whoever was around you at the time, "Didn't you hear me calling you?" and they always say they didn't hear you. No one knows why this happens, and you don't know how to get it off of you; all you can do is pray that God will let you up.

Ricky wasn't the only one things were happening to at this new house. One evening as my daughter, Rough, Ricky, my 2 year old granddaughter, and I were in the kitchen. She was swinging a toy bat like she was playing baseball with someone. We looked at each other, and I said, "Who she is playing with?" Thinking nothing of it, my daughter and I resumed what we were doing. My granddaughter kept swinging the bat, and the next thing we knew, she put the bat down, started crying, and wanted to be picked up. She wouldn't talk, and at that point we knew she had seen something. We assumed she must have realized that she shouldn't be playing with whatever it was. A few minutes later, she was talking again to herself. I honestly believe that she saw things all the time. When she was smaller, she would look out the window all the time and smile. I also believe that the spirits lived upstairs because that is where most of problems would occur (in the bedrooms).

One day my granddaughter was in her bedroom playing. I heard her talking to someone or something and having a full-blown conversation as if someone else was in the room with her. I called her name, but she didn't answer. I called her name again and got the same response. A few minutes passed, and I decided I should find out why she suddenly stopped talking and wasn't answering me. Before I got up, she came into my room and said, "Yes, Grandma?" I asked, "Who was you talking to?" She said, "My friend." I said, "Your ..." and she appeared scared and ran to her room. I went to her and asked if they told her not to tell me, and she nodded yes. I explained to her that she didn't have to be scared to tell me. She simply said okay and resumed playing.

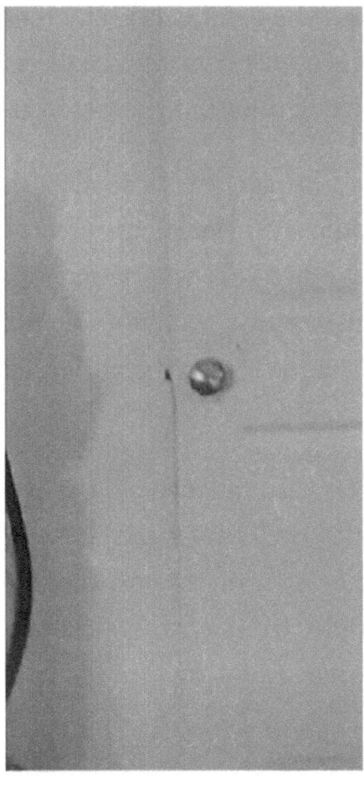

Ghosts

MY GRANDSON IS AWARE OF WHAT is going on, and he even helped in an investigation, but now he too appears to be scared. At one point my grandson wasn't very verbal. During this time, he would often run around and holler, "Ghost, it's a ghost." We took it very seriously because he had not been very verbal and did not have much of a vocabulary, so we couldn't figure out where he had gotten the word ghost from. Better yet, how did he know what it was? My daughters went to the school to ask the teachers if they had possibly talked about ghosts because Halloween was coming, and they said no. They hadn't started working on their Halloween themes yet.

We kept a close eye on him, paying close attention when he would say ghost. At times he would even wake up screaming, "Ghost!" I asked my daughters, "Does he act this way when he is sleeping at home?" They said no; they only saw this behavior when they were at my house. I did not want the spirits to hurt my grandchildren or tell them to do anything bad.

Now that grandchildren's are older, we have explained to them that if and when they see things they know aren't the "norm" to not be afraid and to let an adult know as soon as possible. I am so happy that they are older and know right from wrong. It makes me feel a lot more comfortable knowing that they won't be easily influenced by whatever is going on.

Humming in the vents

TINKERBELLE MOVED IN A COUPLE OF years ago. She never had any problems until now. Lately unexplainable things had been happening to her as well. She had only heard us talk about the things that went on but never had any personal experiences in my home. Her peacefulness, however, soon came to an end. Tinkerbelle was going to take a shower to get ready for work when she heard a woman's voice humming through the vents. She paused, wondering if what she was hearing was real. She resumed washing and then heard this peculiar humming again. She stepped out of the shower, wrapped her towel around her, and went to see if the television or radio were on in her bedroom since no one else was home. Once she discovered there was nothing on, she became afraid to proceed with her shower. But she did and hurriedly dressed and departed for work. She called me from work to tell me that she heard a lady humming, and it seemed like it was coming from the vents. I had never experienced this, but I also did not think this was the beginning of a crazy journey of experiences for Tinkerbelle.

Voice

THE NEXT DAY KID WAS IN the upstairs bathroom and heard a voice whispering, "Mom." He yelled, "Hello, hello," because he knew I was still asleep and everyone else had gone to work, but there was no response. So once he finished in the bathroom, he entered the bedroom and woke me up, asking if Rough had been there a few minutes ago. I said, "No, not that I know of." He turned and headed to his side of the bed, realizing that if she had been there, she would have responded to his call. With a confused look, he said it sounded just like Rough whispering "Mom." He got under the covers, and neither one of us mentioned anything else about it.

Why?

IT SEEMED LIKE THINGS STARTED HAPPENING to us when we were in the bathroom and alone. One morning I was in my bathroom upstairs, standing in front of the mirror, when the soap came flying past me from the ledge in my shower. I asked out loud, "Why are you doing that? Leave me alone."

The following day Thumbs was downstairs in the bathroom when a shampoo bottle came flying at her. I couldn't believe what she was telling me, knowing what had happened to me the day before. I was in complete disbelief. I told her what happened to me, and she was speechless. She said she didn't know what was going on or why they had started to mess with her.

A few nights earlier she was sitting in the TV room watching television, and her arm began to burn. Not knowing where the burning sensation had come from, she looked down and noticed that there were three scratches on her arm. Rough and I were in the kitchen preparing dinner when she walked in and said, "Oh my God, look! There are scratches on my arm. It just started burning, and I looked down and saw these." When she held out her arm, there were long marks that looked like someone had scratched her, except no one could have done it because she was there alone.

At that very moment, I felt a strong presence in the kitchen, and a shadow appeared in the doorway. I turned to be sure my peripheral vision wasn't playing tricks on me, and for sure there was a shadow disappearing around the corner. I kept it to myself for was very familiar with what I saw. In fact, I often felt that same presence when I was in the kitchen. But just like tonight, every time I looked all I would catch was a glimpse of this mysterious shadow either disappearing around the corner or sort of gliding by the kitchen as if it were passing by. Focusing my attention back to what was going on, I simply said, "Okay, now I have to figure out something because they are showing signs of possibly harming us in here." I knew at that moment I had to get someone out to my home to find out what was going on and what we could do to put an end to this madness before someone or me got seriously hurt.

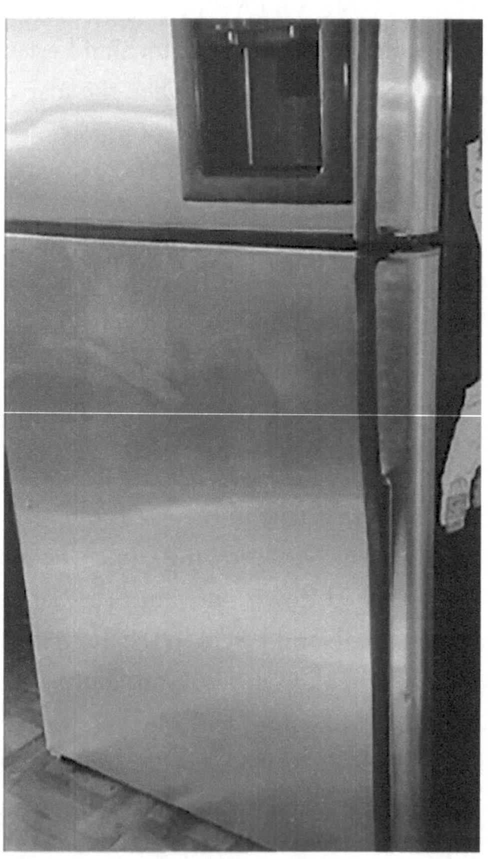

Spirits

IT WAS ANOTHER LATE NIGHT FOR Rough and I. We were sitting in the kitchen, and Rough said, "Oh my God, Mom, something is in the hallway." I said, "Something like what?" She said, "It's a man." Tinkerbelle and I gazed at each other with an empty look because we had no idea what to say or do. She said, "Hurry, come now and see." We jumped up, and by the time we got to the hallway, nothing was there. I said, "Rough, were you playing?" She said, "No, Mom!"

He was about my height, appeared to be African American, and wore a white shirt and jeans. She also stated that he was bald. This was the first time that anyone, including me, had seen something that was clearly in a human form, and we didn't know why it was in this house. We always saw dark figures or shadows or just something passing by, but nothing this clear. I was kind of glad that I didn't get to see head on what she was describing. I know I would have been terrified to the max. And she talks about the man on a horse the horse is white he is a white man. I haven't seen the man on the horse, but I can hear the horses outside.

Husband

ONE EVENING I HAD COME HOME from work and was sitting on the edge of the bed taking off my uniform. Suddenly the covers moved as if something was under them and moving up the bed. Kid was sound asleep. I knew this because he got into bed as soon as we came in and began snoring. Still I turned around to make sure he was fast asleep, Never mind that he was lying on his stomach; he was still as ice, and his arms were stretched over his head. Once I confirmed that he was sleeping and these covers were really moving, I flew off the bed, stood firm on my feet, and I screamed at the top of my lungs, "Kid, get up!" As he jumped up, he asked groggily, "What, what's wrong with you, Tyin?" I said, "There is or was something in the bed with you." He said, "What? Where?" Flipping through the covers (while I stood there impatiently waiting for whatever was going to come out from under there at any moment), he came back with nothing. I was so terrified that I was completely speechless.

Once his search came back clean, I think he realized what had me screaming like a madwoman. Being used to the unexplainable events that had been occurring lately, he looked at me, shook his head, and got back in bed. He eventually dozed off. I was so scared to get in the bed that I just sat there until I couldn't hold my eyes open any longer. Then I slowly climbed into bed and finally drifted off to sleep.

Dead Spirits

AS I OFTEN DID WHEN I didn't get right up for work, I hit my snooze button and drifted back to sleep. I'm not sure how long I must have slept after my alarm went off at 8:00 a.m., but I smelled this awful aroma. It was so awful and smelled so bad that I think it's safe to say it smelled of something dead—and after it had been dead for a while at that. I jumped up knowing no one had died in my house and thinking perhaps one of the kids was downstairs burning something. So I yelled, "Who's burning something?" I got no answer. I yelled again. No answer. I got out of bed to see what was going on downstairs only to find out that no one was cooking anything, and I also noticed that the smell wasn't downstairs. As I went back upstairs, I realized the smell was gone. I called Kid and asked if he had smelled something (and described the smell to him) before he left for work, but he said that he hadn't.

This was not the first time that something unexplainable woke me up when I was running late. Outside of the smell and the whispering in my ear, they had also touched my ear, and when I woke up, I noticed I had overslept. I'd just say thank you and make sure not to show fear and go on about my day, assuming they were possibly being nice by waking me up. We all hear a voice calls out our names sometime when you home alone or we all can be home like you will hear ma I would answer, and they would say no one called you. This happen to all of us in the house.

It can be difficult to get people of expertise and experience to come to your home, especially once you explain the things that go on.

And because of my circumstances, I couldn't get a soul to come and investigate my house. But I didn't stop looking. Some churches charged one hundred dollars to come out. I never called any Catholic churches, but I did go to different places asking for help. The churches didn't know what to do because no one had come to them for this before. I was told to call some paranormal services, so I start looking them up. I called two teams, but only one made it to my house. A man came out to see what he had to do. He was scared; you could see it in his face. He said he would bring back his team, but that never happened. He called and said he was coming, but the spirits blocked him. And they blocked the other team from coming as well. I couldn't take it anymore.

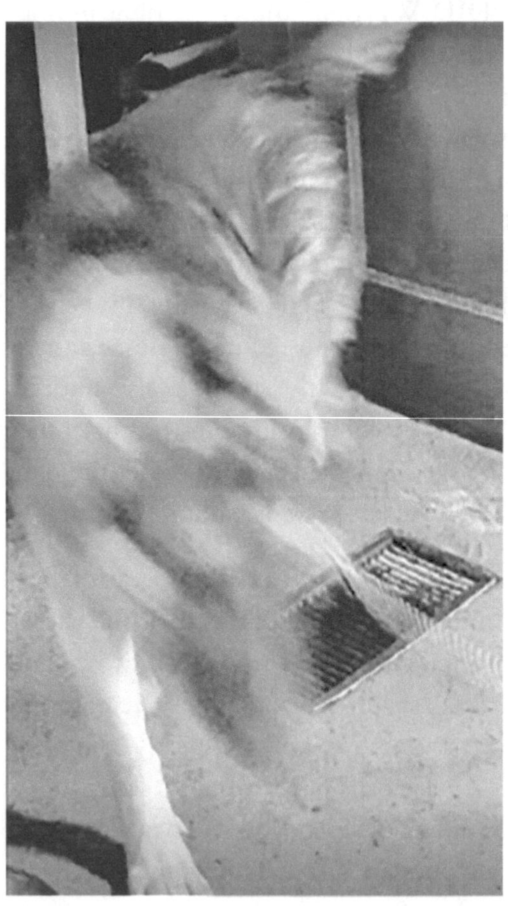

Bishop and Wife

I CALLED MY OTHER SISTER AND told her what was going on in the house. She called a coworker, who was a bishop, and told him the situation. He called me, and I asked him if he had dealt with this before. He said yes, he had. I think maybe it was more than he could handle because this was not a small problem. But we set a time and date for him to come and bless the home. The bishop arrived with his wife, and I don't think she knew what she was getting into. He didn't know either but was willing to try to get them out.

When the bishop came into the house, he knew something was going on. He could feel them. He started upstairs because he said the spirits were living in my son's room. Then we began to hear things moving around in there. The bishop went in the room and prayed. It was hard for him, but he did it. You could see he didn't like what he saw because he was rushing. When we got to the basement, it was a different story. His wife was scared, and he was too. The bishop started praying, and next thing I knew he was speaking another language of a demonic spirit. We all were scared, and his wife was terrified. We didn't know what to do. He stated that he couldn't do this and invited us to come to his church. I went once, and then I never saw him again. My sister sees him and his wife, but they never ask her about the house. I kept on looking and calling different places.

Paranormal Team

I FINALLY GOT HOLD OF A paranormal team that agreed to come out and do an investigation. They wanted to come at night since that was considered "dead time," as they called it, and they would more than likely capture more stuff. I agreed that they should come around nine or ten o'clock. They called when they were about five minutes from my home; they couldn't find where we were located because their GPS system went out as soon as they turned on Ritchie Road. So my daughter had to guide them to our house over the phone. Once they got to the house, their GPS system came on again right before they turned into my driveway. They couldn't believe that the system had gone out for it had never done that before. They came inside and started getting out their equipment.

Before they could even begin the investigation, things started happening. They went in the basement to set up, but the electricity went out. Everything upstairs, however, was still fully working. Once the electricity came back on, they were able to hook up the equipment, but their cameras lens would not capture the scenery. The screen was pitch black on both cameras.

I had left Rough in charge because I didn't get off from work until 11:00 p.m. She called me both excited and nervous about what had just happened. I told her everything would be fine, just be careful, and I would be home shortly. When I got home, they had finished setting up, and they wanted to start in the basement alone. So my three daughters, my son, two of the paranormal team members, and I stood outside talking, and they asked me to fill them in a little bit more about what went on in my house. As I was doing this, my youngest grandson screamed, "Ghost!" My youngest grandson had a ideas of what they was here for and was very helpful at the time and what the people were doing there. The team wanted to know what he was excited about and started to question him. His vocabulary was limited at the time, and he knew very few words. The female team member asked him, "What do you see? Where is it?" He replied, "Ghost, the boy and the water." She asked him to show her where the boy went. He walked to my Rough's car, which wasn't working but just sitting in the yard and pointed under the car on the passenger's side near the tire. The team member told my youngest grandson to tell the boy "to please go into the light." Although he didn't have the words and wasn't able to put words together independently, he was able to mock pretty much anything he heard. So he repeated on demand, "Go to light." Then he said, "He's gone," and resumed playing with his toys as peacefully as he had been before he spotted the boy. The team member suggested that the boy in fact did go into the light.

Two of the team members were mediums, and they came outside shortly after that to tell us we could join them inside for the rest of the investigation. The female team member briefly told them what had happened. She said, "her youngest grandson just said he saw a boy, so we told him to tell the boy to head to the light," and he did because she no longer felt his presence. The medium stopped right there, held her throat, and said, "I feel like I'm choking on water, like drowning. There was a little boy; he drowned over there in a pool." This shocked the heck out of me because we never mentioned anything about the water part, and I had told her nothing about my land or neighborhood. She knew nothing about my neighbor's land being occupied by a pool years ago. She said it was good we sent the spirit into the light for he had been lost for a long time.

Just minutes after this happened; Ricky's cell phone began ringing. He said, "Ma, I'm right here; why are you calling me?" Once he came around the car and saw I didn't have a phone in my hand, the look on his face was of pure horror. He said, "Where is your phone?" My phone was sitting on the front porch. I asked my daughter Tinkerbell to get the phone, and when she bought it to me, the screen was black and still locked. There was no way I could have made that phone call. I told him, "Do not answer the phone!" My daughter's phone then started ringing, and her caller ID said I was calling as well. When we looked at my phone, the screen was still black. I told her the same thing: "Do not answer!" At this point the team members told us to answer the phone. So, we did, but it was just static on the other end. When I asked, "What do you want?" it hung up. We all gathered in a circle and waited to see if the phones would ring again, but they didn't, and we went on with the investigation.

Thumbs feared these things no matter how much we tried to convince her that she would be fine. So she decided that she wanted to be part of the investigation, hoping it would help her to not be afraid of these kinds of activities. We headed up to my bedroom to get started, and Thumbs sat in a lounge chair. The paranormal team was not having much luck in my bedroom at first, but soon they were picking up on things, and their equipment went crazy, especially their EVP recorder for ghosts hunting catch their voices and hear what they are saying to you. While this was happening, Thumbs started saying ouch. The pain was so bad that she was nearly bent over out of the chair. "My ear, my ear, something is wrong with my ear," she said. We told her to hurry out of the room and get downstairs to the rest of the team until we finished upstairs. As she was going downstairs, the team was running up the stairs to try to see what was behind her. It was a spirit, ghost on camera reaching for her. Once we got downstairs, Thumbs described the awkward pain as something sharp going deeper and deeper into her ear. She was scared to death. But the pain stopped as soon as she got to the table with the paranormal team. It was crazy.

The paranormal team produced some interesting findings. They were able to get in touch with five spirits in my home that day. They discovered an older man, a little girl, and two women, one in her late sixties and one in her late twenties. They also discovered a man in his thirties. The women expressed that they were afraid of the older man. We wondered if this was the same male figure that my daughter often saw standing around. The paranormal team wrapped up and went back to their headquarters to collect their findings and told me they would be in touch with their results.

Once they had them, they called and said they wanted to meet; they had something I needed to hear. They let me listen to all the tapes they had from a few nights ago. One of the men was very communicative and said his name was Arthur. He was asked if they could take a picture, and he replied sternly, "No pictures!" He stated that he found comfort in my basement, and that is where he spent most of his time. We were careful not to disturb anything. He stated that he didn't want us to take any pictures of him again we did ask why not? No answer. He said he live here and been here for a long time and he wasn't leaving. At that time, we granted his wish then another spirit came in and said he like pictures like to party.

We were shocked and nearly overwhelmed by these results, all of which verified my assumption that something was going on in my home. I couldn't thank them enough for coming out and assisting me because we really needed help. Anytime ghosts, spirits mess with kids you need to get somebody anybody to come where ever you are to protect them from harm. And for everyone because they can hurt you, make you hurt yourself, or kill you, and make you hurt or kill other people's. I think it's safe to say it is better safe than sorry.

About a week later we met with the team again to learn some things we might do to get them to leave our house. They came and tried to force them out with no luck. They gave me house-cleansing methods. No luck. They scheduled to come out again, but they never showed. Then it seemed as if something happened. The team just vanished. They stopped answering when I called. They never returned my messages, and I haven't heard anything from them since.

It's almost as if something ran them off.

Black Magic

THINGS WERE HAPPENING AND SEEMED AS if they had sped up again. So, I was back at square one. I decided to try to find someone else or possibly another team that could come out and help me. As my frustration continued to grow, I decided to lay off the search because it was beginning to mentally and physically drain me.

There was a young man who was a friend of my son's. Because of their closeness, he soon became a friend of the family. One day he was visiting us, and we was discussing spirits in general. Pete said, "My house is haunted. Black magic was practiced there." So I asked him to explain. Pete stated that he thought it started with his aunt, who practiced black magic, Long ago when his father was hospitalized, his aunt was visiting and said that all his father's sons were cursed. The aunt later died, leaving the house that she had built. She didn't leave it to her only brother; she didn't like him. And Pete's father didn't want the house. He was sick of the stuff she was doing to him his sister. His mind wasn't right, and he couldn't do anything but sit at the table.

This house was very small and sat back off a long, country-like dirt road. There was no neighbors in sight. Soon Pete and his family started experiencing various paranormal activities in the house. Strange things were happening all the time. One of the stories he told involved cats. A lot of black cats is bad luck. There used to be ten black cats lingering around the house. They didn't know where the cats came from and chalked it up to living in the country. Maybe these cats were strays and liked their land. One day Pete decided to gather all the cats and take them far from his home and leave them there. Later that night, as Pete was arriving home from work, he pulled into his driveway where he saw ten estranged black cats like those he had dropped off earlier that day. They appeared to be waiting for him. He said that he was terrified to get out of the car and go into the house.

He said that as time went on so did the weird experiences. There were black snakes that usually "hung out" on top of the house. One night as Pete and his little brother were lying in the bed, they heard a loud, fearful but familiar scream. "Mom," they both yelled as they jumped out of their beds and ran into their spiritual mother's room. They were nearly out of breath, gasping for air, and speechless. She pointed under the sheets to a black snake. Pete yelled for his father, who also resided with them, and he managed to kill the snake and remove it from the house. Pete also experienced things like black shadows standing in the doorway of his bedroom; they appeared to be men wearing long, black trench coats. Pete had a Bible that he wanted to bring to the house, hoping for some type of comfort, but for some reason something did not let him take it into the house. It was almost as if every time he was about to take it in, something would grab hold of him.

As Pete was driving home one night, he was traveling along the dirt road to his house, and as he looked in his rearview mirror, each lamppost light turned off one by one as he passed them. When he finally got home, he was so scared to get out of the car that he called inside the house to his brother and asked him to come out and meet him.

Similar things and experiences kept happening. So, in desperate need of some help or advice, he came to my house and was discussing his experiences with me. As he was doing so, the lights in my house went completely out. Everyone came downstairs to see what was going on. I said maybe we should all go outside until the lights came back on. As we were finishing up our conversation, the outside lights and the lights inside starting flickering on and off, and a heavy breeze began to blow. The breezes suddenly stopped, the outside lights came on and stayed on, and the inside lights came back on. Pete and his brother went home, eager to try the new methods that I told him about. The next morning Pete called me, ecstatic. He said that they did everything I suggested, and things were looking brighter already. They slept peacefully the night before, and they felt refreshed in the morning. They haven't reported anymore stories!

Pete has since met someone, had children, and moved out of his parents' house. Of course, things were still happening in my house, and nothing had changed—with shadows, missing items, and unexplainable events. I've talked to psychics and readers and asked them to come out, but no one will check out my house.

Spiritual Mother Contacted

ONE NIGHT WHILE AT WORK I was having a conversation with a coworker about his similar experiences. I decided to tell him a little about what had been going on with me and that I was having no luck with assistance. He began writing and said, "Here." He handed me a piece of paper and told me to call this woman, and that she would surely be of help. I gave her a call, and she agreed to meet with me. I went to her house, and my daughter and I got a reading. We had told her nothing, but she gave a very accurate reading and told us practically everything about us. I was impressed. She told me about the spirits in my house, which I had not mentioned to her, and said she was coming to my house. She began calling to check on me and inviting me to her house and to church on Monday nights. We established a bond that remains inseparable. We call her Spiritual Mother at her request. She did a spiritual cleansing of my home. We felt much relief after she did the cleansing; it even seemed different after a night's sleep in the house. It felt more refreshing when we woke up. She stated that although she got the spirits out of the house, they would remain on my land—it was formerly a plantation—because they considered it their home too. She said if they weren't in the home, we would be fine inside, but she couldn't put them off the land. This was fine with me if they weren't inside with my family and me, especially around my grandchildren's.

Sex/Kill

ONE DAY SPIRITUAL MOTHER WAS AT the house. She had never met my oldest daughter Tinkerbell and started talking to her. She asked questions, such as "How do you feel in the mornings?" and "Do you feel a bit strange?" My daughter was in shock, wondering how she knew that. In fact, we all were because a week earlier my daughter had come to me and said she often felt weird, especially when she woke up in the morning. It was almost as if something was having sex with her in her sleep. Although my daughter and I knew what she was hinting at, we remained quiet and continued to listen carefully.

Spiritual Mother told her that a male spirit was attracted to her, and to make the situation worse, he was practically in love with her; he lusted after her. He wanted her sexually, mentally, and emotionally. He was so in love that he often had sex with her at night. She stated that this was dangerous because my daughter could end up with a "spirit belly." Sort of like a pregnancy, it could possibly result in death. This kind of spirit was called an incubus male demon/spirit that has sexual intercourse with a woman. She also said he felt that she was his woman; she was his wife, so to speak. Spiritual Mother suggested that my daughter allow her to perform a cleansing and work on her with some things that would keep him away from her. We reluctantly agreed and set a date for her to do the cleansing, and she also gave us a list of things we needed to get for that cleaning.

We went to her on a Friday evening and got the work done. She stood Tinkerbell naked in a tub and went to work. She began to pour all types of ingredients on her from head to toe, including liquor, coconuts, limes, vinegar, and water, washing her hair and body in it all. She was told not to bathe or wash her hair for the next three days. She performed it and gave her a ring to place on her finger and a few simple instructions to follow, along with a verse to read daily. She also gave her something to drink day and night for the next three days. We had no idea what Spiritual Mother had mixed up in the bottle. Tinkerbell described it as the most awful, nastiest thing she'd ever tasted. After following these instructions for a week, she began to feel relief, and she began to sleep peacefully. It had been two months since the cleansing was performed. She hasn't had any problems since and reports to sleep very peacefully at night.

Spiritual Mother said she wanted to perform something at my house that was sometimes known as "calling them (the spirits) out." I agreed. She tried to get some of her friends to assist her. People would agree to come out with her and then cancel the day before; this happened three times. It was almost as if they were afraid to come, or something was prohibiting them from coming. After numerous attempts she finally found some help, so she came out and brought two of her accomplices with her. She suggested that we come together in prayer before she did anything. We did this, and then she began to do what she came for.

She drew a circle on the floor with symbols on the inside of it using baby powder. She asked if we had a mirror, possibly the biggest mirror in the house. We gave her a mirror that used to be on a dresser, and she placed it in front of her on the floor. She began asking questions, such as "Why are you here?" and "Why are you bothering this family?" and "Why won't you go into the light?" When they answered, it was almost as if Spiritual Mother began to turn into another person. Her voice deepened tremendously, and she started to rock back and forth. At that point she became one with the spirit and became the spirit, and she allowed us to ask the spirit any questions we might have. Through Spiritual Mother the spirits began telling us what we needed to know. They stated that they liked places like the basement and the kitchen. They mainly liked the kitchen because that was the common meeting place for the family, and they often spent time there drinking and mingling. She instantly snapped out of it and said, "Do you all see her?" Although we didn't, she explained that there was a beautiful, young-looking lady in the mirror. She was also able to learn that there were four children in the house. We later learned that the older man and the young lady were married, and they had four children. We also found out that the husband had killed the wife. The wife was afraid of her husband, and Spiritual Mother said he was a very mean spirit. He told us that he was not leaving the house. We also learned that he was the one who was infatuated with Tinkerbell; he was also the one causing the most havoc in the house. I think it's safe to say that Spiritual Mother has since then gotten him out of the house, and we haven't had any problems with him since.

Although we may still experience little sightings here and there, possibly a shadow or a passing figure, we haven't had any major problems. Spiritual Mother continues to work with us, trying to get all the spirits and experiences down to a bare minimum. Every time she does her work, we truly can feel a change. We has since formed a relationship outside of "business" and consider each other family. She has been sincerely dedicated to working with us until my home is completely peaceful and free of spirits and unwanted guests.

Ricky

ONE AFTERNOON RICKY WAS IN HIS room playing a game as he normally did on his days off from work. He was home alone. I had hurt my hand on the job and was out on leave after having surgery on my hand. I had to go to therapy twice a week. On this day I was at therapy, and everyone else had gone off to work. There was a knock on the door. The knock was so light that Ricky paused his game to make sure he had in fact heard a knock. Then the knock happened again. Unsure of who could be knocking on the door because he wasn't expecting anyone, he went to open it. No one was there. He stood curiously looking, and after confirming that no one was outside, he decided to close the door. Just as he was closing the door, it dawned on him. Could he have in fact opened the door and invited someone—worse yet, something—in?

I returned home from therapy, and he told me what had happened. I told him he should not have opened the door if he didn't see or hear anyone answer him. I called Spiritual Mother to see what I should do, and she simply stated in her strong accent full of love and care, "Don't worry, darling, I'll be there."

Sister Nono experienced something in the beginning in July. She was sitting on the couch watching TV, and she felt something pull her hair. A few days after that happened, she was getting dressed and decided to take a picture of herself. When she looked at the picture, she noticed a lady standing in the mirror next to her. I've noticed over time that her facial features have changed into a demonic form. My sister Nono liked to play around and dress up like an old lady. And that day she was taking pictures and the lady in the mirror was in the pictures too.

My niece was over one day. She had heard us talking about the spirits in my home many times, but I don't believe that she believed what we were saying—until that day. She was taking pictures of herself, and when she went back to look at them, there was a ghost in her photos. She called me, and she was so scared. She told my sister Lamoya her mother that she didn't know what to do. She sent the pictures to Rough and I. Then she told me she would never come to my house again, but she has been back. But not like she used to.

Sheila

SHEILA WOULD COME OVER, AND THINGS would start happening to her and her kids. She has been pushed down the stairs and scratched and bruised all over her body. She would show us what happened to her. These are violent and demonic spirits we are dealing with. The spirits said they like violence, drinking, smoking cigarettes and fights in the home they are trying to cause problems in the home because I won't do what they want me to do move out. I said I was not moving; they had to go. This was my home now, not theirs anymore. They would do anything to make us scared of them and to anybody who came to my home. Some guessed they had seen them in dark shadows passing by or felt something sitting down beside them. And they would ask, "Did you see that?" or "Did you hear that?" and no one would say anything.

Sheila couldn't sleep in Rough bedroom because something would always happen to her. She would ask for a different room, but there was no space. She would go in the basement to watch movies, and she would see things. She would be so terrified that it would make the kids scared to move. They would run and hide because they didn't know what to do. They were scared to answer the door and wouldn't tell you someone was at the door. The ghosts would show themselves to the kids, and they tried to explain what they saw; they were terrified. Spiritual Mother was called again.

Sheila knew what was going on in the house, and she was scared. I didn't know what to say to her. I didn't like what I was seeing. I was scared too. In the basement she was typing, and the laptop began typing on its own. You could see the keys typing. She was screaming and hollering, and we all ran down there; we all saw it. No one thought to record it. Even if we had, we would never see it again because everything disappeared. Some pictures did appear in a family member's phone. She could see the ghost; she could tell you what it had on and what it looked like. We didn't say much because we all knew no one would believe us.

Playing in the Basement

THE KIDS WERE IN THE BASEMENT playing; they would go down there every day to play. Suddenly they were running up the stairs. They saw something, and they were scared to death. They were so afraid of what they saw that they were too afraid to tell me. None of the kids would go back to the basement to play. Instead they would ask somebody to go with them to get some toys to play with. They would not go alone anymore. I had to tell them that they couldn't show the spirits any fear. "So try not to be scared because the spirits will keep messing with you if you are showing fear."

The spirits no longer cared who saw them. Ricky and some family members were in the basement one evening, playing games on the Xbox, and things started happening. They asked Ricky, "Is there a ghost down here?" And he didn't know what to say; he was embarrassed to tell them.

Although Ricky hates for me to say anything about the spirits or tell people about them, he knows what's going on in the house. You can see them in the driveway, in the backyard; the lights outside go on and off when they pass by. And at the neighbors' houses, you can hear horses and talking.

Sheila Daughter sweet pea

SHEILA DAUGHTER SWEET PEA TOLD A little kid who was over one day not to go in the basement because there was something down there, but the little kid didn't understand what she was saying. I heard her saying it. I asked her why she would say that to her friend. Then I asked her if there was something down there that she was scared to tell me about. She said, "Nana, yes, there is something down there." I used to be embarrassed, ashamed, and uncomfortable. But I had to be strong because everybody in the house was so scared. I was scared, but I felt like keeping all this to myself would kill me. So now I don't have a problem with talking about it most of the time because this is real. Some people will believe you, and some people will think you're crazy. You can hear a lady singing through the vents in the house and something knocking at the door. We doesn't answer the door because looking to see who is there because if we open the door and no one is there we just let them in the house.

Nephews

TRIGGIE WAS ASLEEP, AND WHEN HE woke up, there was a ghost (a man) in his face.

He called his spiritual mother and told her what he saw. He was so frightened. And his brother, BJ, got up one morning and found scratches on his neck. BJ was asleep another day and woke up crying and very sick, saying his chest hurt. He had sharp pain in his chest and was only eleven or twelve years old. He couldn't breathe, and we thought he was having a heart attack. I gave him some medicine, and the racing of his heart finally stopped. The spirits were attacking him, but his spiritual mother was praying. That's when everything went away.

I was in the kitchen, and my phone was ringing. It was my nephew calling me. I went to him and asked, "Why are you calling me? I am right here." He stated that he was not calling me because he didn't have his phone with him. The phone was in the bedroom, and no one was in that bedroom. I told him, "Your phone is calling me." I showed him my phone and asked him to get his phone. We both went to the room, and he got his phone out of his book bag for school. There was nothing on his phone that indicated he had called me. Later I asked to see his phone again. He went to get it, and the phone was gone—I mean gone. We couldn't find the anywhere. About three weeks later, my grandson came over.

Grandson

I WAS NOT HOME AT THE time my youngest grandson came over. When I got there, he said, "Hi, Grandma. Here is your phone." This was my nephew's phone that I had given him, and it had gone missing. I asked my grandson where he found the phone, and he wouldn't answer me. Then he said, "In the couch." I asked how he knew it was my phone, and he wouldn't answer again. So I asked him again, and he got very angry and said, "This is your phone, and I found it." I went to ask my daughter Rough, his mother, to ask him how he knew it was my phone. He told her the same thing: "That is Grandma's phone." Something was telling him not to tell us, and he wouldn't.

He is a very special grandson; he can see spirits, and he talks to them. There is one, a little boy that he talks to all the time. He has said to us that this spirit boy tells him to do things like hurt his spiritual mother because the boy doesn't like her. My youngest grandson had started talking back to her and wouldn't do what she asked him to do. He would say, "I am going to hurt you." So thumb told Rough what he was doing, and rough is his other mother / god mother he called her Boo. His mother could hear him talking to the spirit, saying, "No, I am not going to hurt my mother. Leave me alone." He used to be scared of the spirits, and some he still is, but it depends on what kind of spirit it is. He will go in the basement and stay all day now. You wouldn't know he was down their unless something bad came in that really scared him.

Rough

ROUGH IS MY DAUGHTER, AND SHE has a gift of seeing spirits. She doesn't like it at all. She doesn't know why she has this gift, but what is she supposed to do? I can see them too, and I get feelings about people and their spirits. My daughter Tinkerbelle has the same gift as I do. The only thing we can say is it's a gift from God. The little boy that my grandson sees came to Rough and told her what he was going to do to my grandson. This boy was in Rough's room, and she had to go toe-to-toe with this spirit. She was not scared of him, but she didn't like what he was saying about her son. She was trying to figure out how to save him from this ghost's violence. My youngest grandson can see them; he talks to them. He called that one boy his imaginary friend who told him to do things to his spiritual spiritual mother. When he told the spirit boy he was not doing it, the boy got angry. This boy could be dangerous to my grandson if we didn't do something.

We are talking to someone who might be able to help with this problem. Rough's jewelry's, rings, keys and sunglasses and other things. The ghosts took her rings off her fingers you just can't take the ring off you have to use force to get it off. We looked everywhere for them, and some days later the rings showed up in her work bag and sometime in the bathroom. Most of time they will give it back put it in places that you wouldn't think to look. She had not been to work. Rough went to sleep, and the next morning something told her to open her eyes. Her TV was off; instead there was the spirit of a man and something else in her TV. She took a picture of it, and it appeared in the photo. She called her brother Ricky and asked him to lay on her bed. He was scared at first, but he did it. At first, he didn't see the spirit, but then he saw it in the picture. The ghosts don't like Rough; she intimidates them, we were told, and the white male spirit is not scared of her. The lights go on and off, and they stay off for about ten to fifteen minutes and come back on. They keep doing the same thing over and over only in that room. And sometimes it occurs with certain people who enter that room.

TV

MY SON RICKY AND I WAS seated in the TV room talking. He stopped talking and looked at something. I asked him what he saw, and I asked him twice. Then he said he saw a spirit floating in the air. I told him I had never seen that, and I didn't like it. About two weeks later, one of my nephews said to me, "Auntie, what was that?" I said, "You saw something?" He said yes, and he was scared. I asked him again, "Did you see something?" He finally said something black was floating in the air. I asked him where it went, and he said in the living room. That was the same thing Ricky saw. I told him it was nothing, so he wouldn't be scared. But I knew what he saw so I called Spiritual Mother and told her what was going on. She didn't like what I was telling her. She said, "That isn't a good spirit" and she would have to come over. Spiritual Mother is like a mother she is not my mother. She has many gifts just to tell you something she can do. She is a medium who can see and talk to the dead. Feel their energy, she can cast out demonic spirits. She is a pastor she loves helping people she a very very sweet lady She has been a big help with getting these spirits out of my house. But they do come back after two to three months, and there might be more new ones. Most of the time it's new ones that come back, not the ones that were here. They can come back as good spirits or demonic spirits, and they can do physical harm to you. They want us to move out. They say this is their home and want us out, and they were told we aren't leaving.

Demonic

GHOSTS OR SPIRITS, WHATEVER YOU'D LIKE to call it, did things to my grandson.

He said a ghost slapped him in the face. He came running out of his room scared and crying, trying to tell me what happened to him. He was eight years old. He was trying to push me in the hallway, telling me to go into his room. I was scared to death. When a ghost hits or scratches you or anything else, it means it is a demonic spirit. This is a very bad spirit that can really hurt you or kill you. I didn't want to go in there because if you don't know what you are doing, you can get hurt or open doors for other things to enter.

I tried to turn on the hall light, but I couldn't let my grandson knows I was just as scared as he was because I wasn't sure what all had gone on. I went to his room, and he was with me, terrified. He didn't want to go back in there. I said to the ghost, "Don't touch my youngest grandson ever again." I asked it to leave my home. "I rebuke you in the name of Jesus." I think my youngest grandson felt a little better, so he got into bed and went to sleep. I stayed in the room while he slept, and I stayed up because I was scared. Sometimes you will hear knocking at the door, walking around upstairs and downstairs, the microwave door closing, and talking. They like to play in my hair.

Pretty Lady

THIS LADY WOULD GET ME UP in the morning. She would say with a soft voice,

"Get up. It is time to get up." I would get out of bed and think to myself, who was that? I was the only one home. If she didn't get me up, I would have been late for work, and she knew that. I believe she was the lady in the picture on my phone. I had been taking pictures, and on one photo this pretty lady took up the entire frame. She was not in my house. She was a black lady with long pretty hair, brown skin, and an attractive smile. I showed the picture to my daughter. She had been in the kitchen with me when I was taking the pictures. I have never seen that picture again; it disappeared from my phone.

A lot of pictures that I have taken with my phone are just gone. Late at night I would take pictures in the house and look at them the next day or a few days later. That's when I would see things in the photos. I have caught a lot of things on them like all sizes of orbs flying around and sitting on the couch or the floor. Dark shadows hiding in some parts of the house are very creepy. The house is haunted, and the ghosts has a lot of activities going on. You will smell sweet perfume, rotten odors, or cigars. There is a man who sits in the corner of the kitchen wearing an old hat and a long black coat. He was standing over us in the background of one picture. The person who took the pictures was so scared that she got rid of them before giving me copies, and she has not been back. I can feel them following me and coming up or down the steps behind me. Sometimes I do feel fear come over me, and I never felt like that before.

Upstairs Hallway

WHEN YOU CAME UPSTAIRS, THERE WAS a shadow in the corner by my bedroom door and the bathroom. A dark shadow was there all the time when my son started to see things too. He now sees the dark shadow in the corner and can feel the spirits, which he couldn't at first—or didn't want to. At one time he would ask me if I saw that or heard that. He told me his TV would go off every night at three o'clock in the morning, and it would wake him up. When the TV went off, it would come back on, and you would hear things going on in his room, such as walking, knocking things over, and opening and closing the door. We would be sitting and see the door open and close. Sometimes it sounded like fighting, and no one was there, and it happened again when he was in his room. Ask them did they hear that in the room, and they said no, but we did downstairs.

Phone text

NOW THE GHOST'S PLAYING WITH MY phone, calling, texting, and leaving messages. And it's not me. My phone will hang up on someone if that person is talking about the spirits. They won't let me call out or get incoming calls, but later I am able to use my phone again. My phone has texts family saying things that didn't make sense like leave, don't come here. Sent family members pictures to their phone of ghostly/spirits pictures that I had in my phone and kept sending them repeatedly.

Sweet Pea

I PICKED UP SWEET PEA ONE day from school because she was sick. We got home, and she went to sleep after taking the medicine she needed. About forty-five minutes later, I went to check on her, and she was up by the fish tank in the living room. I called her name several times, but she wouldn't answers me. I then yelled her name. She answered me, saying she didn't know and peed on herself. I could tell by her face that something had scared her.

The following day we had a guest at the house. I heard her tell the children not to go in the basement because something was down there. The kids did not understand what she was saying. I asked her why she would say something was down there. She was scared to answer me. With a blank looks on her face, she replied, "Yes, there are spirits in the basement." I asked her not tell people because it would scare them like it scared us.

Running

THE DOG WAS TRYING TO RUN from them. They were making him face the wall, and he licked in the air as if they were giving him something to eat. One night he was hollering and trying to get away. I told Kid to get up and see what the ghost was doing to him. Pooty stopped hollering and seemed frightened. I think they were hitting him. So I prayed and asked them to get out of my room and leave the dog alone. I noticed that I had to do this often when it came to Smokey.

The following week, the kids (who lived in the house) were in the basement playing. The next thing I knew, all of them were running upstairs. They saw something that had them very afraid, but they wouldn't tell us what they saw. They don't like to play down there too much anymore. Now they just go down and get whatever they need and run back upstairs. Now when they must go in the basement, they usually ask one of the adults to go downstairs with them.

The spirits don't care who sees them anymore. Ricky and friends of the family were in the basement playing games and just hanging out. Things started happening, and his friends asked him if there were any ghosts down there. Ricky didn't know how to respond. I think he was ashamed to tell them what was going on.

Girls Night

SOME TIME HAD PASSED, AND THE spirits were quiet, so I decided to have a girls' night. I went around the house taking pictures, mostly of the basement. When I went back to look at the pictures after a day or two, I noticed spirits in the mirror and large and small orbs flying around. You could see faces in the pictures, as well as books and hats. You had to pay attention to what was in the pictures because you would see things that weren't there. And if you had never experienced spirits before, it could terrify you, after taking the pictures, we watched movies and had a good time. We went to sleep, but we heard voices, and some of us were being scratched. A lady whispered softly, "The lights are going out in the bathroom." I knew what was going on, but I didn't want to say anything. I knew if I did, everyone would leave. Some family member knew what was going on, but no one said anything. I know they were happy to go home.

Spiritual Mother

I CALLED SPIRITUAL MOTHER AND TOLD her I needed to see her. She told me to come over the next day. When I got there, a friend of hers also was present. I told Spiritual Mother about the pictures, and her friend asked to see them. I didn't know that she could see things. She showed me that ghosts were in all ten of the pictures, and they appeared to be alive. There was a man with a hat on, and a lady in the corner behind the basement door had her fingers to her lips like she was saying, "Be quiet." Spiritual Mother told me that she needed to come to the house.

On October 20, 2016, at 8:30 p.m., Spiritual Mother and three of her friends came to the house. They all had gifts. One lady came in but had to leave for a few minutes. The spirits immediately began talking to Spiritual Mother, and she stated that there were a lot of kids in the house. One ghost told her that this house belonged to them, that they wanted my family to leave, and that we all should have been dead. They then said to let them stay, and we could live together. They wouldn't bother us, and we wouldn't bother them. They asked if we could put some teddy bears out for the kids to play with. I told them there would be no more cooking in the kitchen and turning up while we were cooking. They also had to leave the kids who lived in the house alone, as well as anyone who came to visit us.

I have a little house in my backyard, and Spiritual Mother said that was where some of the spirits lived and that the white man who used to live in the house wanted all the spirits to live in the house out back. I know there had to be at least one hundred different spirits in my home. The land used to be property of a plantation. The white man asked Spiritual Mother if she was going to come back and try to run them out. He was told she might because she was not scared of him, and he knew it. He said he had to call a meeting with the other spirits, and he would let us know.

Spiritual Mother told me that they weren't going to leave because they thought this was still their home. I told the spirits that this was now my house, and my family was not leaving. They started making everyone who lived in the house angry and fight with one another. They wanted us to draw blood because they wanted someone to die. This is what they told me. These things continue to happen. I'm going to have to have Spiritual Mother come back because Rough is angry, and she doesn't know why.

On November 1992, my dad passed away, and on that date I got a package in the mail. I was asleep, and Kid put it on the bed. When I got up, I looked at the box and thought, I didn't order anything from JC Penney. I didn't open it and went on about my day. Later I asked everyone in the house if they had sent something to me, and they said no. So, I decided to open the box. One of the spirits had sent a ring, a beautiful ring. I contacted JC Penney so they could track the order and see who sent me the ring. The agent got the tracking number from me and said they didn't have any such order in the system. No one knew who sent the ring. I called my sister-in-law and told her what happened, and she said that was strange. As of this day, we still don't know where the ring came from.

Kid seems to think the spirits are following me because my dog Smokey didn't have any problems when I went on vacation. I prayed over him before I left. When I came back, he started up again. He was scared to go outside and was knocking things over and trying to hang himself. He tried to get under me, afraid to move. So, when Kid told me how Smokey was when I was gone, I prayed over him. He seems to be fine for now, but it's going to start up again.

It was strange what Kid told me about Smokey because on that ship I could feel something was following me. I could hear it walking behind me on the ship. I kept telling my sister that it felt like something was walking behind me. At some point I did feel fearful, and it was the first time I felt like that on any ship. I was scared; I wanted to run. I feared my own shallow. I would try not to think about it, and I didn't tell anyone how I really was feeling. I prayed all the time on the ship because at that point the spirits might have killed me, and no one would have known what happened to me.

I have been told that there are spirits following me from place to place. I have seen spirits/ghosts all my life, and the only thing I didn't know was that they could hurt you, kill you, and make you kill or hurt yourself. I have seen some things that ghosts can do to you. They can start fights and make you violent. It is real. It is not a joke. People have ghosts in their homes and don't realize it.

I have been trying to get this book done for some years, but the spirits blocked me from writing my stories. They broke every keyboard I had, and I bought ten. I had five different people trying to type for me, and not one completed my book. Everything would disappear as if nothing had been typed or the typist hadn't save it. I typed with two fingers to get this book finished. The something that was happening to them was happening to me too. It was hard to write this book in the house because the spirits blocked everything, including everybody who tried to type this book for me.

I have proof of some things on CDs with the spirits' voices saying things, as well as in some pictures. I ordered a paranormal investigation. I was going to try to investigate myself, but I didn't because something was telling me not to do it. I had to find someone who knew what they were doing because if you don't know what you are doing, it could be dangerous and open doors that you don't want opened. No one will believe you if you tell them this is happening to you. I know because when I started telling people, including family members, they didn't believe me until some of them saw for themselves. Then they believed me.

I don't care who doesn't believe me. I know what I see, hear, and smell, and what they can do to you. The only thing I can say is maybe one day you might experience or encounter the same thing. Until then never say it's not real because it is.

My father passed away in November 1992, and my mother passed away in February 2012. They knew everything I was going through. Both saw spirits/ghosts. They would always try to make me feel that it was nothing so I wouldn't be scared. It helped, but it didn't as I got older and things got worse. My mother didn't likes this house. She wouldn't come over too often, and if she did, she wouldn't stay long. She helped me with this book and was proud of me for even trying to write it. I didn't let anything stop me from finishing it. May both of them rest in peace. Love you

ME

I HAVE PRAYED AND ASKED JESUS to send my father, my mother, and whoever else wants to come and build an army to help me get these spirits out my house and away from my family and me. Jesus can do it alone; he doesn't need help. I have asked Jesus to take these ghosts and spirits out of my house—to please make them leave, keep them away, and stop them from wanting to attack us and making everyone in the house angry and violent. Enough is enough with this mess. So I am asking, please help us with this. I am asking in Jesus's name. In Jesus's name I pray, in Jesus's name I pray, in Jesus's name I pray. Amen, amen, amen, amen.

Recognize

PEOPLE ARE BEGINNING TO RECOGNIZE SUPERNATURAL and paranormal activities. It is all over the television, in movies, and even on the internet. People are coming out and telling their stories. Don't hold it in; let it out. If people assume or think that you are "crazy," so be it. You may have experienced things that others haven't experienced, but that does not make you different. Only God can give you these gifts. I believe seeing spirits is a gift. They do exist, and it is in the Bible. Ephesians 6:10-12 Acts 19:13-16. Leviticus 19:31

If they didn't, I would not have taken the time to write this book. Things started happening to me in my early years, and they are still happening to me today.

www.ingramcontent.com/pod-product-compliance
Lightning Source LLC
Chambersburg PA
CBHW030351200726
48286CB00013B/1074